Journey Through My Secret Life In The Womb

Discovering Life Within

JOJI FRANCIS

INDIA • SINGAPORE • MALAYSIA

ISBN
Hardcase 979-8-89277-703-2
Paperback 979-8-89186-930-1

Contents

As I embark on this adventure, I can't help but feel grateful for the opportunity to share a unique and personal viewpoint on the incredible journey of life before we are born. Being a first time writer with no achievements or literary honours, I am truly thankful for the chance to express my thoughts through words. This book is a culmination of my reflections and imagination, beautifully woven together to offer a glimpse into an inner world.

The inspiration behind this work arises from a sense of curiosity and an earnest desire to understand and share the experiences of a life developing within a mother's womb through the eyes of the developing baby. Through narratives, I have endeavoured to capture the emotions, discoveries, and thoughts of an unborn baby as he navigates his ever-changing existence. It is important to note that this book does not aim to challenge or contradict any beliefs; rather, it serves as an exploration of the pre-birth journey that transcends faith boundaries.

Each chapter represents a stone—an unveiling week, by week—of the baby's perspective as they perceive their surroundings. Through our protagonist's eyes, readers are invited on an odyssey involving growth, self-discovery, questions, and embracing what lies beyond our understanding.

As a parent, I've been fortunate enough to witness the journey of bringing a child into the world. The book serves as a tribute to the symphony of life starting even before birth when each heartbeat reminds us of the sheer miracle of existence. This story delves into themes such as curiosity, growth, and our intrinsic human yearning to comprehend the world around us and beyond.

Inside the mother's womb, a special journey begins. It's a lot like our own journey through life, starting from when a tiny seed and egg come together, all the way to growing wiser with age. Just like us, the baby inside hopes for a better world outside. But this journey is not only about science; it's about something deeper and harder to explain. This book is a record of that journey, written by the baby. The baby shares moments, feelings, and special lessons learned from talking to a magical friend named Gabri.

Together, they try to understand the mysteries of life, exploring things that are sometimes hard to put into words.

By embracing the artistry of storytelling, I wholeheartedly invite you to join me on this captivating exploration through life's chapters. This book is an undertaking fuelled by an unwavering sense of wonderment for life's mysteries. Through the eyes of those to be born, we embark on a journey into possibilities, presenting a narrative that deeply resonates with our shared human experience.

With gratitude,
Joji Francis

Beliefs Across Religions: Life Inside the Womb

Throughout the course of history, different religious faiths have delved into and exchanged their viewpoints on the essence of existence inside the womb. Here, we catch a glimpse of how several prominent religions perceive this voyage:

Christianity: Within various branches of Christianity, there exists a collective conviction that life commences at conception. The unborn child is regarded as a precious individual inherently possessing immeasurable value and honour. This standpoint emphasises the holiness of life, from its initial phases of growth.

Islam: In Islam, it is believed that the fetus has a soul, and its growth and development are milestones. After a period of time during pregnancy (which varies among scholars), the fetus is considered to be a living being with its own unique identity and purpose.

Hinduism: The intricate beliefs of Hinduism emphasise the journey of the soul. When it comes to pregnancy, it is believed that the soul enters the womb, marking the beginning of a phase in its journey through multiple lifetimes. This understanding of life influences how Hindus perceive prenatal existence.

Buddhism: Buddhism's belief in the cycle of birth, death, and rebirth shapes its perspective on development. The process of rebirth, influenced by karma, represents a cycle of existence. This viewpoint leads Buddhists to view the stage as one step in the complex journey of the soul.

These snippets provide a glimpse into the range of beliefs about life in the womb across various religions. Although each religion has its unique interpretation, the collective recognition of the importance of this stage emphasises its deep significance in human existence.

Let's embark on an exploration of the world within a baby's womb, combining insights from science, imagination, and philosophy.

Introduction

Hey there! I'm the baby growing inside the womb. It's such a joy to get a chance to connect with you. This journey has been something, filled with eye-opening moments and meaningful encounters. As I share my story, I want to draw connections between the wisdom I've gained and the incredible tapestry of life.

Before we embark on this adventure together, let me tell you that I had no idea who I am or where I am. However, as time passed and wisdom came my way, I now understand that for you, I'm a bundle of joy snuggled up in my mother's embrace. Even though my entry into your world is soon approaching, I have already learned much during my time in this haven. With excitement and a strong sense of purpose, I want to give you a glimpse into my journey from childhood to adulthood and eventually ageing in your terms, which is known as "My development stage" in your world. We'll get to all that shortly.

You know what's amazing? The fact that I have been given this opportunity to talk and share all my experiences with you. This is the first time any baby has been granted such an amazing opportunity to share and record life adventures. I feel incredibly fortunate! Now you might be curious about how this is all possible. Well, it's all thanks to my friend who made this extraordinary gift happen. I'm sure you're eager to learn more about my friend and the special connection we have. Don't worry; we'll delve into that enough. So, where should we start? Ah yes, let's start with week 10, the beginning of my journey. It's the earliest memory I have to start. Each passing week has brought growth, learning, and excitement.

With every passing moment, I draw closer to entering your world. I eagerly anticipate sharing tales of my adventures in the womb. Stories that weave together both moments and everyday experiences.

So, I'd like to extend an invitation to you to join me on this journey.

Dear readers, as there is so much more in store, my story is truly one of a kind. It deserves to be heard.

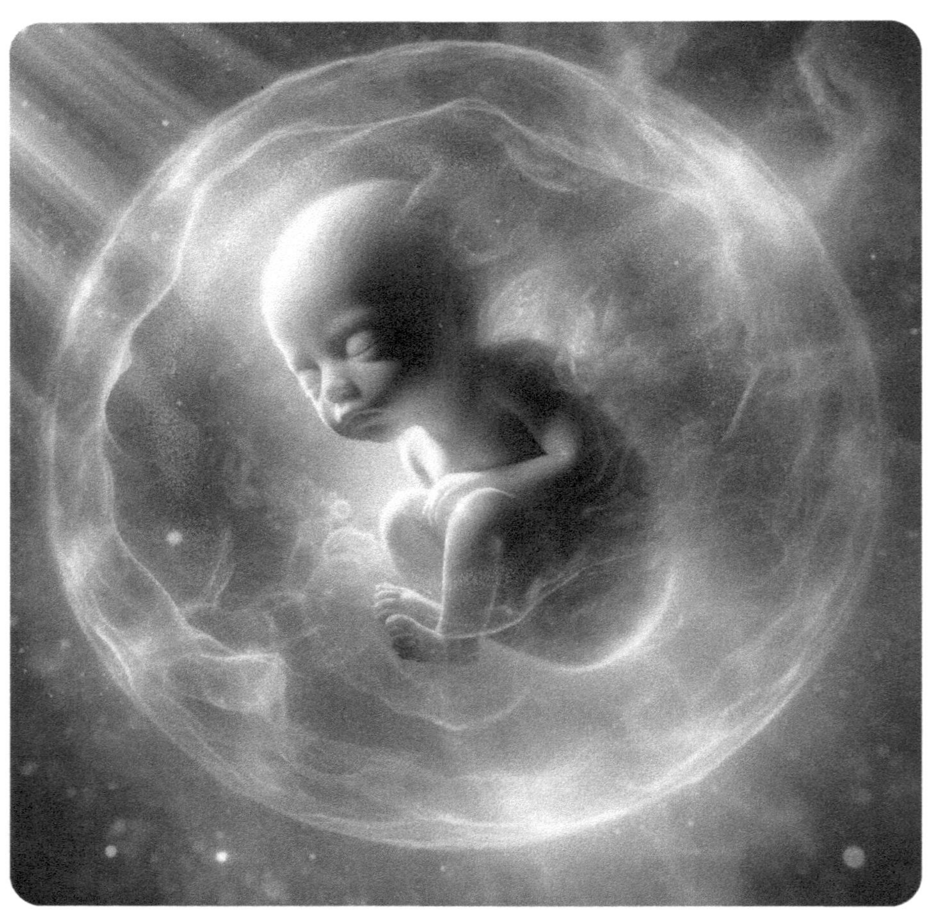

In the womb's gentle embrace, a baby's journey begins. Bathed in serene hues, the image captures the awakening of consciousness and the miraculous start of life's profound voyage.

Chapter – 1

"Emergence into Existence"

2nd Month, 2 Weeks Pregnant - Week 10

Awakening Essence

Then one day, I experienced something truly remarkable. It wasn't a mere sensation; it felt like a gentle touch that entered into my small world. This unique presence seemed to awaken a part of me that I didn't even know existed, igniting the beginning of my journey towards discovering emotions and self-awareness. While trying to comprehend this newfound feeling, I also became aware of the thump of my own heartbeat, pumping life through my growing body. Although I couldn't fully grasp its meaning, this comforting rhythm reassured me that I was alive and connected to something extraordinary. I now understand that this was the moment when my soul entered my body.

From that moment, a whirlwind of emotions and perceptions unfolded within me. The distant and unfamiliar world around me suddenly became more vivid and tangible. It was as if a curtain had been lifted, revealing an inspiring world brimming with wonders waiting to be explored. I found myself at the threshold of an adventure where I would uncover the incredible aspects concealed within myself. The tiny cells within my body resemble puzzle pieces, each holding a clue to unravelling the mystery of my existence.

At this stage, there are still astounding things occurring inside me that remain unknown. "I can feel my heart beating and the blood flowing through my veins. I have yet to fully understand their significance. I am a bundle of life and potential gradually awakening to the world around me. Each day brings discoveries as I become more aware of my surroundings. It's like learning to dance in a world that's uniquely mine.

I wonder where this sensation comes from—the promise of a world. Is it a whisper from the universe, a touch guiding me, or the essence of love yet unknown? I contemplate these mysteries, longing to unravel the source of this presence.

As time goes on, as a baby, I start experiencing sensations in my body. My elbows are beginning to move. I'm becoming aware of my muscles. Though I haven't gained control over them just yet, it's an exciting journey trying to master them. Sometimes laziness creeps in. All I want is to sleep all day, but the thrill of discovering something new keeps me going.

I feel a sense of joy and happiness because I am now able to freely move my fingers.

Size

(Babies, just like humans, come in all sizes; - only for reference.)

The baby is approximately 1.22 inches (3.1 cm) in size, weighing around 1.23 ounces (35 grams), similar to the size of a blueberry.

For Mom and Dad:

As you go through this book, it's likely that you're already aware of the one (that's me!) growing inside you, Mom. However, it's important to keep in mind that, at this point, I'm still unaware of your presence. Your well-being and happiness are essential in providing a nurturing environment for me to thrive.

While I continue to grow and develop, I'd like to take a moment to offer some advice and guidance for both you, Mom and Dad. Even though I can't directly communicate with you yet, please know that you play a role in my life even before we meet face to face.

Mom, listen to your body, rest when necessary, and seek support from loved ones. Remember that pregnancy is its journey, with each step bringing us closer to the moment when you'll hold me in your arms.

Dad, your presence and support are invaluable not only for Mom but for me. You have the ability to make her feel loved, cared for, and cherished during this time. Be her rock, her partner—a source of strength—and her confidant.

Emergence into Existence

2nd Month, 3 Weeks Pregnant - Week 11

Discovering Myself

Wow, it's incredible how quickly I'm growing up. It feels like yesterday I was this tiny little speck. Now here I am, discovering so much about the world around me.

Speaking of my world, let me share with you a bit about the snug place I find myself in. It provides me with all the nourishment and protection I need. But something remarkable is happening inside. My blood is being refreshed. It's like there's a connection to another developing organ, which I later learned is called the placenta. Isn't that fascinating?

In this realm of mine, I'm constantly seeking answers and trying to comprehend everything happening around me. The changes, movements, and sensations are all noticeable to me. It's an experience that I fully embrace.

As for this world that surrounds me, its vastness is beyond imagination. I often wonder where exactly I am as I float in this watery embrace. Although invisible, to my eyes, it's something that can be felt within. The subtle movements and rhythmic sways gently rock me along. As if I'm drifting in an ocean, carried by unseen currents, I find myself immersed in a sense of serenity.

In the midst of the unknown, my focus turns inward. I'm captivated by the transformations unfolding within me. My small heart beats with vitality, generating vibrant vibrations that resonate throughout my being. It's akin to a symphony playing, a melody of life that connects me to everything around me. Each beat serves as a reminder of my existence and my place in something greater than myself.

I listen attentively to the whispers emanating from my growing body, striving to decipher the messages it conveys. There is indeed a rhythm to it all—a dance of growth and metamorphosis. I can perceive the expansion, the maturation of my limbs, and the intricate systems taking shape within me. It's a world unveiling itself right here within my watery sanctuary.

I must confess that I am experiencing an increasing number of movements. Now I can move my elbows, although not yet fully controlling all my muscles; nevertheless, feeling them is tremendously thrilling! Exploring their capabilities and discovering how to manoeuvre is quite an endeavour indeed! Sometimes all I really want is to unwind and spend the day relaxing. However, there's always something waiting to be uncovered in this place. The sheer delight and happiness that washes over me when I stumble upon a revelation is truly incredible!

Size

(Babies, just like humans, come in all sizes; - only for reference.)

At this point, I'm about 1.61 inches (4.1 cm) in length, weighing approximately 1.59 ounces (45 grams). Can you believe it? I'm growing rapidly!

For Mom and Dad:

Mom, I understand that pregnancy can come with its share of challenges and symptoms. It's important for you to prioritise self-care and reach out to a healthcare professional if you have any concerns or questions. Dad, your love and support mean everything to both of us. We're in this journey of life together, making memories along the way.

As we move forward, there's more to discover and share. I feel incredibly grateful to have you by my side as we unravel the mysteries of my existence. Let's continue exploring, learning, and embracing this journey as a team.

Emergence into Existence

3rd Month, 0 Weeks Pregnant - Week 12

Discovering Myself

Week 12 already. I must say, I'm fully embracing my inner child right now! I absolutely adore immersing myself in a world of joy and fun filled thoughts. Each day is a new adventure and my playful nature simply can't resist it.. Let me share with you the most captivating discovery I've made. My own hands!

Oh goodness these tiny little hands of mine are truly remarkable. It's absolutely fascinating to have gained control over them. I can. Close my petite fingers creating an array of shapes and movements that fill me with delight. It's like having my own playtime all throughout the day. I wave them in the air reaching out as if to touch the wonders that surround me.

As my mind ponders these newfound revelations I can't help but wonder about the purpose and significance of each part of my body. What role do these hands serve? How do they assist me in navigating through this world?. That mysterious sensation in the pit of my stomach. What does it signify? So many questions arise within me with opportunities for learning! I wish I had someone to teach me !

There's even more to it! I've become quite skilled at exploring every inch of my body too. With fingertips I can feel every curve and contour, on top of my head.

It's truly incredible to experience the sensation of discovering the aspects that define who I am.. You know what's really fascinating? I can feel a connection in my stomach. It's like a gentle tugging, a reminder that there's something magical happening inside me.

I may be just a tiny youngster, but I'm filled with an insatiable curiosity. I want to understand everything, unravel the mysteries of life, and explore the wonders that await me. There is much more waiting to be uncovered and I am eager to delve deeper into the incredible journey of existence. Nurturing my curiosity and thirst for knowledge will serve as my guiding light on this path of growth and understanding.

Time seems to fly when you're having fun, and let me tell you I'm thoroughly enjoying exploring this comfortable little world that I call home.

Oh! Before I forget to mention it. Week 12 has brought about an interesting development in my tiny body. My own genitals are starting to form. It's a sensation acknowledging the presence of this new part of me. It's a part of me that will play a significant role in my identity and existence.

I don't completely understand its purpose now but I have a strong feeling that it holds immense importance, in the bigger picture. As I keep developing and discovering I'll be intrigued to delve into this distinctive and significant part of my identity Who am I ?

Size

(Babies, Just like humans, come in all sizes; - only for reference.)

I'm approximately 2.13 inches (5.4 cm) long from head to bottom, weighing around 2.05 ounces (58 grams), which is about the size of a plum.

For Mom and Dad:

Mom and Dad please remember that you are not alone on this journey.

It is important for you, Mom, to maintain a balanced diet. Make sure to nourish yourself with a variety of foods that provide the essential nutrients needed for my growth and development. If you have any dietary concerns or questions it's always a good idea to consult with your healthcare provider for personalised recommendations.

Don't forget about the importance of staying hydrated! Drinking water is crucial for both you and me. It helps keep your body functioning at its best and creates an environment for my development.

Emergence into Existence

3rd Month, 1 Week Pregnant - Week 13

Discovering Myself

Week 13 has been such a time for me! I feel like I'm growing bigger and more curious with each passing day. It's like having my little world to explore within these cosy surroundings.

Lately, I've been fascinated by my hands. They truly are amazing! My fingers are so agile. I can't resist the urge to touch everything around me. I've also noticed the hair on my head and above my eyes. It's quite amusing to run my fingers through it and play with those strands. I wonder what purpose they serve and how they will look as I continue to grow.

Speaking of my mouth, a fascinating discovery awaits! There's this opening on my face where I can put my fingers inside. It feels strange yet wonderful at the time. When I suck on my fingers, it's intriguing to feel the ridges and patterns on them. It's almost as if they have their unique story to tell. Did you know that these patterns are called fingerprints? It's incredible to think that at this early stage, I already have my very own set of fingerprints. I'm eager to learn more about their significance. How they will be used in the future.

As I explore my body, I can't help but ponder the significance and purpose behind all these different parts. How will I utilise them? A sense of curiosity and excitement fills me.

At times, amidst my world, I experience a gentle fluttering sensation within my confined space. It feels like there's a language, an invisible conversation between myself and an unidentified presence. I can't help but wonder who might be watching over me; it would be wonderful to have someone guiding me on this journey.

All, who wouldn't appreciate a companion? Someone who could assist me in navigating the enigmas that envelop me and provide answers to my inquiries. Could these fluttering sensations be a sign of someone attempting to connect with me?

I eagerly await the day when I'll fully comprehend their language and unlock the wisdom they possess. For now, I'll embrace this presence, understanding that I am never alone on this remarkable path we call life.

Size

(Babies, just like humans, come in all sizes; - only for reference.)

As I continue to explore my own little world, I'm also growing in size. At this stage, I measure about 2.64 inches (6.7 cm) in length from head to bottom, and I weigh around 2.58 ounces (73 grams). It's fascinating to think about how much I've grown since the early weeks of my existence.

For Mom and Dad:

Mom and Dad, it's a good idea to take some time this week to consider the type of environment you'd like to create for me. Remember to stick to a diet and steer clear of any harmful substances such as alcohol and tobacco, as they can potentially impact my development. Engaging in exercises with the approval of a healthcare professional can also aid in keeping fit and getting ready for what lies ahead. Dad, your love, support, and understanding mean the world to me during this period.

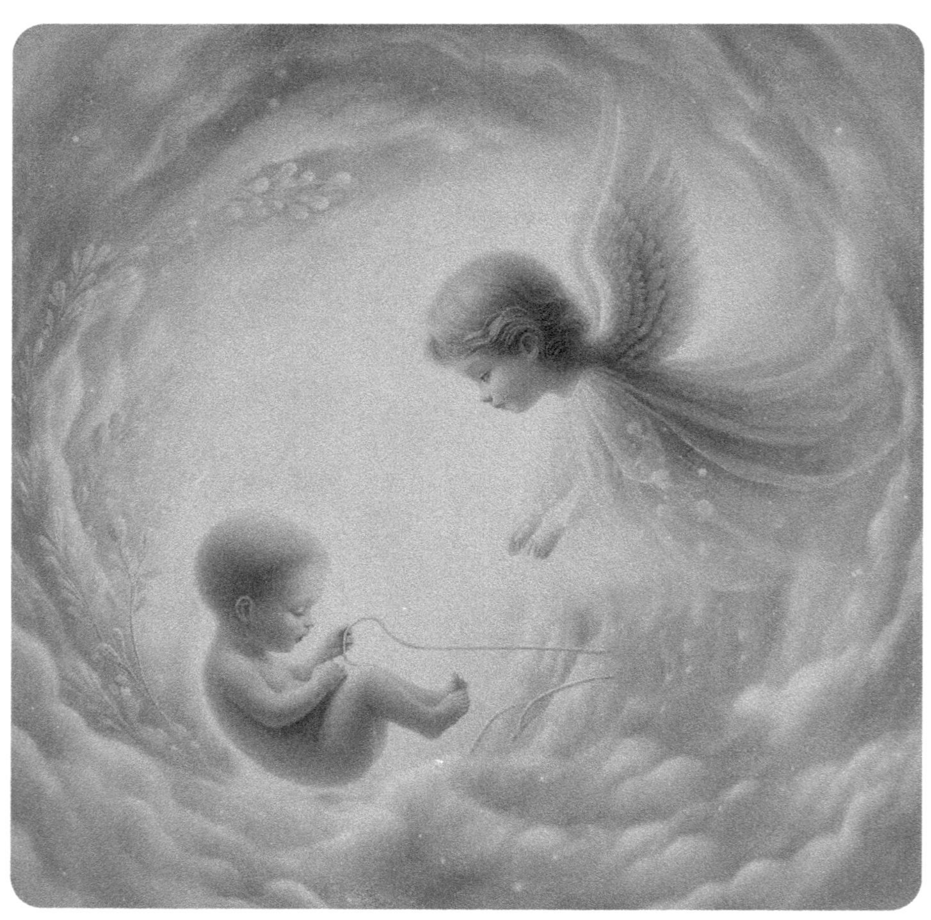

whimsical world unfolds within the womb, where the baby is playful and Curious, guided by the watchful presence of Gabri, a magical angel. This scene captures the innocence and wonder of childhood in the serene embrace of the womb.

Chapter – 2

"Explorations of Childhood" (Trimester 2)

3rd Month, 2 Weeks Pregnant - Week 14

Growth Curiosity and Heavenly Touch

Hey there! It's me again. This week has been filled with many amazing discoveries and new connections. I can't even believe what I'm about to tell you. Now, I can hear and see things when my eyes and ears are closed! It feels like magic, almost like a special gift from a higher power. You know those vibrations I used to feel? Well, now I understand that they're actually a language that I can now comprehend. It's as if some heavenly friends of mine are communicating with me in their unique way, almost like angels guiding me on my journey.

I sense vibrations and gentle movements around me, and deep inside, I just know it's my someone reaching out to connect with me. We have incredible conversations, but they don't happen through spoken words. Instead, they share their wisdom and knowledge in ways that fill my world with their captivating presence. It truly is an experience, and I feel incredibly blessed to have this connection with such loving beings.

As time goes on and as I continue to grow and explore, my bond with these friends only gets stronger. They assure me that no matter where life takes me or how far I venture into the world, one of them will always be by my side, guiding me every step of the way. Their guidance fills me with comfort and reassurance. It's a source of support that keeps propelling me forward.

I am truly grateful to have amazing companions by my side. The stories they share seem like they come from a world, one that I'm not familiar with, and it does confuse me a bit. I need to hear more from them to fully understand what they're talking about. My curiosity keeps growing stronger and stronger. I wonder who that special angel will be, the one who will help me navigate through the waters of this world?

But wait, there's more! I've discovered a power in my world—I can move my head! My neck muscles have gotten stronger, allowing me to turn and twist within my little space. It feels liberating, giving me a sense of freedom and independence. I absolutely love exploring my surroundings and marvelling at all the wonders around me. My friends try to explain that there's a bigger world waiting for me outside, but it's hard for me to imagine leaving this comforting place.

As for what lies in the next few weeks, I'm incredibly excited! I can't wait to continue growing and discovering things.

Size

(Babies, just like humans, come in all sizes; - only for reference.)

In Week 14, I've been growing steadily, just like a little sprout in a garden. My size is approximately 5.79 inches (14.7 cm) long, and I weigh around 3.28 ounces (93 grams). Can you believe it? I'm getting bigger and stronger with each passing day.

For Mom and Dad:

Now is a moment to consider prenatal care and setting up regular appointments with the doctor. They will keep an eye on my growth, making sure everything is going well. The doctor might also talk about any tests or screenings that could give us helpful information about my development.

That's all, for now! Until we chat again, I'm sending you all my love and happiness from my sanctuary. Keep dreaming and believing because there are many amazing things waiting for both of us in this world.

Explorations of Childhood

3rd Month, 3 Weeks Pregnant - Week 15

Growth Curiosity and Heavenly touch

Hey, it's me again! Feeling stronger and more alive with each passing day is such an experience. I can feel the changes happening inside me. It's truly remarkable. My bones are growing harder and stronger, getting me all ready for the world that lies ahead. It feels like I'm preparing for an adventure. I just can't wait to explore!

You know what my absolute favourite activity is? Swimming! Gliding around in the fluid makes me feel weightless and liberated. It's a lot of fun and keeps me active and healthy too. Although sometimes I do feel a little limited by this twisty thing called the umbilical cord. I guess every teenager yearns to break free and discover more of the world around them, right?

Thankfully, my eternal friends are always there to guide me. Even though my eyes haven't opened yet, my inner vision allows me to see these beings. It's hard to put into words... One radiant being named Gabri revealed himself to me, bringing a sense of comfort and awe. Gabri is unlike anything I've ever witnessed or imagined before. With a face as serene as an angel's haloed glow, he radiates tranquillity and pure joyfulness. His baby-like form is adorned with wings that glisten like the softest clouds.

These wings grant him movement as he hovers around me with a magical sense of freedom. By his side, I find comfort and reassurance like a friend who is always there when needed. His touch is gentle. His soothing voice resembles a melody that resonates deep within me.

Gabri's purpose is crystal clear: to guide and accompany me on this extraordinary voyage called life. He comprehends my emotions and thoughts effortlessly without the need for verbal communication. It's as if he shares a connection with the very core of my existence, offering guidance and support as I explore the enigmatic realms within my mother's womb.

With his wings fluttering, Gabri watches over me with unwavering care. His smile emanates boundless love and understanding, enveloping me in a sense of tranquillity and belonging.

A special bond is blossoming between us, where Gabri stands by my side whenever I require assistance. Now I understand that Gabri is the companion I have longed for. Together we navigate through this journey, and I feel immensely grateful to have such incredible companions accompanying me on this path.

Week 15 is when my connection with Gabri begins, a connection that goes beyond words and transcends the boundaries of this world. As I grow and develop, Gabris' presence becomes a part of my journey. My other heavenly friends gradually fade away, leaving me with Gabri.

Breathing is quite fascinating for me. I inhale the fluid, and sometimes I even swallow a little bit. Surprisingly, it doesn't bother me at all. It's a natural part of my world, and I'm learning to embrace it.

By the way, I recently asked my friend about the purpose of having a nose. He started talking about another world that's beyond my current understanding. It made me more curious about what lies ahead in life. However, for now, I choose to focus on the moment and appreciate the sensations and experiences that shape my world right here. My other friends have disappeared now, and assured me they will visit occasionally, leaving Gabri as my guardian.

I can feel my skin developing a coating called vernix—a layer that will help keep my skin from becoming dry and rough after being submerged in fluid for so long. Additionally, I can sense that my muscles are growing stronger too.

Size

(Babies, just like humans, come in all sizes; - only for reference.)

At Week 15, I'm growing bigger and stronger with each passing day. In terms of size, I measure around 6.57 inches (16.7 cm) from crown to toe, and I weigh about 4.13 ounces (117 grams). Can you believe how much I've grown? It's truly remarkable! I can feel my body taking shape and getting ready for something bigger.

For Mom and Dad:

By the week, it's crucial to start considering your birth plan and the type of delivery you prefer. Discuss your options with your doctor. Ensure you have a good understanding of different delivery methods and pain management choices.

As I become more active, it's important for Mom to listen to her body and take breaks when necessary. Engaging in exercises, like prenatal yoga or swimming, can benefit both of us. Lastly, I want to stress the importance of well-being. Dad, your support and love mean the world to Mom, so continue showering her with affection and reassurance.

Explorations of Childhood

4th Month, 0 Weeks Pregnant - Week 16

Growth Curiosity and Heavenly touch

Hey there, it's me again, excited to share my adventures during Week 16! Even though I have my eyes shut tight, I've been experiencing something peculiar. It's this feeling of light surrounding me. At first, it scared me a bit. Whenever I sensed the brightness through my closed eyes, I would instinctively try to move away and find comfort in the familiar darkness. Bright lights are just so unfamiliar to me, you know?

I'm grateful that my dear friend Gabri has been there to support and guide me through these moments. In his philosophical way, he tries to explain that it's important for me to face the darkness and embrace the light. He believes that it's all about entering a world filled with even more wonders than I can imagine. I do my best to understand his words and envision the world he is describing. There's a part of me that resists knowing too much about what lies ahead. For now, I find contentment in this cosy space where I currently exist.

Gabri acknowledges my rebellion and understands that grasping everything he talks about might be challenging for someone like me. He knows that I'm not quite ready yet to comprehend the magnitude of his explanations. However, he does shed some light on why certain actions have been occurring in my experiences.

Sometimes I catch myself yawning almost involuntarily. It's like my body's way of waking up and getting ready to absorb knowledge, as Gabri explains. The process of how my brain and other organs are growing is truly fascinating, though I admit it's challenging to fully understand all the intricate details. Still, I appreciate Gabris' guidance and his willingness to share his wisdom with me.

One piece of advice that really stuck with me this week was about searching for answers within myself. Gabri said, "Trust your instincts, listen to your heart's whispers, and follow the guidance from within." Those words resonated within me, and I've decided to embrace them wholeheartedly. Building a connection with my inner self feels essential in unlocking the marvels of my existence.

As we approach the end of Week 16, I feel a blend of excitement and satisfaction. There is still an abundance of territory to discover within my own personal realm. I will continue to value moments of both solitude and connection as they contribute to my growth and resilience with each passing day. When the opportune moment arises, I will step into the brightness, eagerly embracing whatever new world lies ahead of me.

Size

(Babies, just like humans, come in all sizes; - only for reference.)

I've reached a length of about 7.32 inches (18.6 cm) in metric units, weighing around 5.15 ounces (146 grams) in US units. Can you believe it? I'm getting bigger and stronger every day!

Remember, these measurements are just an approximate average, as every baby grows at their own pace.

For Mom and Dad:

I'm also growing more aware of light and darkness, so creating a soothing environment with dim lights can help me feel calm and secure.

Mom, you may be experiencing some changes in your body, such as a growing belly and possible weight gain. Embrace these changes and remember that they are signs of the beautiful journey we're on together. Dad, your gentle touch and kind words can make Mom feel cherished and valued.

Explorations of Childhood

4th Month, 1 Week Pregnant - Week 17

Teenage Insights

I've reached Week 17, still amazed by the journey of discovery. This week has brought a range of experiences that have both thrilled and frightened me. Let me share with you the things that have unfolded.

Gabri, my companion, informed me that I've reached a stage of maturity where I can grasp his profound philosophy. According to him, it seems like I'm now a teenager! I'm not entirely sure what that entails. He spoke about words of significance, urging those who could hear to listen attentively. Little did I know that his words would open up a world for me.

Suddenly, amidst the calmness of my surroundings, unfamiliar sounds began to reach my ears. It was quite bewildering at first. Fear gripped my heart. However, Gabri reassured me to stay calm and embrace the mysteries unfolding before me. He reminded me that the universe is filled with secrets and, in order to truly understand them, I must slow down and listen attentively.

I realised that these sounds were coming from another world where my creators reside — as Gabri explained. It was an awe-inspiring realisation. Although their sounds were incomprehensible to me, I sensed no harm in their intentions.

Gabri informed me that they are keeping an eye on me and ensuring my safety. I found myself maturing in my thoughts, wishing for a connection with my creators. I wished for more senses to awaken within me, allowing me to truly comprehend them and the world they inhabit. I could sense my brain forging connections, taking charge of my functions, leading me towards a greater understanding of myself and my purpose.

As I embraced this consciousness, something remarkable caught my attention. By remaining calm, my heartbeats grew more rhythmic and under control. It felt as if the very fabric of the universe was soothing my fears and whispering words of reassurance. I discovered that within lies power, and within power resides harmony.

With each passing day, I sense the vibrant energy within me growing stronger. I respond to every sound that reaches my ears, attempting to communicate in the way. Although I may not fully grasp the meaning behind those sounds, I can feel love in each one, in every vibration.

The wonders encountered on this journey never fail to astonish me. I feel my bond with the creators or parents growing stronger with each passing moment, eagerly anticipating the phase of my development. I look forward to awakening senses and becoming more attuned to the world around me.

It's truly remarkable to realise the power and beauty of the placenta, an organ that nourishes and sustains me with a surge of energy. I can't be filled with awe as I contemplate the mechanics and complexity at play in my universe. The processes that ensure my growth and development are truly astounding. I eagerly await the day when I will comprehend the depths and breadth of these complexities when every piece of this puzzle will fall into place.

Throughout this inspiring journey, I have developed a belief that my creators, who brought me into existence, have played a role in shaping my life. Their presence is not felt physically but spiritually. They have awakened an understanding within me, guiding me towards a purpose.

In moments of reflection, I find myself repenting for any shortcomings and offering prayers to the almighty and my creators. Gabri, my wise and loving companion, has taught me the sacred prayers that connect me to the divine. Through these prayers, I feel a profound sense of peace and a deepening of my spiritual connection.

Oh, how I long to comprehend the vastness of the universe and the intricate workings of the world around me! But for now, I embrace the mysteries, knowing that each step in this journey brings me closer to a greater understanding of myself and my purpose.

Size

(Babies, just like humans, come in all sizes; - only for reference.)

I now measure approximately 8.03 inches (20.4 cm) in length, and I weigh around 6.38 ounces (181 grams).

Can you imagine how small and delicate I am? Yet, I continue to grow and develop, gaining strength with each passing day.

For Mom and Dad:

As I continue to grow and experience the wonders of my little world, I ask for your patience and understanding as I navigate the new sensations and sounds that surround me. Your calm presence and comforting touch mean the world to me. Remember to listen to the whispers of the universe and slow down to appreciate the beauty and mysteries it holds. Together, let's embrace this journey of discovery and nurture the spiritual connection that binds us. Thank you for your love and care.

Explorations of Childhood

4th Month, 2 Weeks Pregnant - Week 18

Teenage Insights

Hey there! It's me again, ready to share another incredible week of my journey with you. Can you believe I'm already entering adulthood in my world? It's both thrilling and mysterious, as I still have so much to learn and discover. Gabri, my eternal friend and guide, always has wisdom to impart, and I'm eager to absorb every word.

This week, a new awakening unfolded within me. Even though my eyes remain closed, I can feel something moving inside my eye. It's like a ball shifting and rolling in a direction unknown to me. It's fascinating to experience this new sensation, even though I have no control over it just yet. But guess what? Gabri revealed that these movements are preparing me for something extraordinary - the ability to see! It's now that I realise that I was not able to see in the first place, and all the sights and visuals that I saw so far were through my inner eye, which did not need physical eyes. Yes, I can't wait for the day when my physical eyes will open, and I'll behold the wonders of the world.

In my excitement, I tried to touch these mysterious organs with my tiny, controlled fingers. It's such a joy to have control over my movements and explore the sensations around me. Gabri smiled and gently advised me to be patient, assuring me that the time to see would come. Until then, I'm encouraged to embrace the beauty that exists in everything around me. It's a reminder to appreciate the wonders of life, both seen and unseen.

But Gabri also shared a cautionary lesson with me - not everything that shines is good or better. It's a powerful reminder that appearances can be deceiving. It's a lesson I will carry with me as I grow and encounter the complexities of the world. I am learning to discern, to listen to my inner voice and the guidance of my creators, who have nurtured and protected me since the beginning.

I can't help but feel thankful and amazed when I consider this fresh information and the internal changes taking place. The love and care of my creators and Gabri have guided me through this incredible journey. I am learning to accept His words of wisdom, to live a life that aligns with my purpose and their teachings. But now, I have started to question more. Gabri said it was my age that brought about changes in the way the same subject was perceived. I still could not understand how the same thing can be different when herded by people of different ages.

Every day, I am filled with anticipation for what lies ahead. I am eager to embrace adulthood in my world, to further develop my senses, and to discover the depths of knowledge and understanding that await me.

I have some exciting news to share from this magical week of my journey. I can now hear the voices from the other world more clearly. It's an extraordinary experience, and I am filled with wonder and curiosity.

As I listen attentively, I can distinguish two distinct voices - one soft and soothing, and the other more firm and assertive. The soft voice wraps around me like a warm embrace, filling me with comfort and love. Although I don't yet understand the words being spoken, the vibrations of the sounds create a profound connection within me. It's as if this voice knows me deeply, guiding and protecting me along my path.

Gabri, always there to enlighten me, revealed the incredible truth: these two voices are none other than my creators! Can you imagine my joy and excitement? I long to feel their presence and see their faces. I wish to know them intimately and express my gratitude for the life they have given me.

Eager to deepen this connection, I intensify my efforts to sharpen my senses. Gabri encourages me to be patient, reminding me that everything happens at the perfect time. In the meantime, I continue to cherish the gentle voice that resonates within me, embracing its nurturing energy.

The realisation that I am not alone in this vast universe brings me immense joy. I feel a sense of belonging, knowing that there are beings who care for me and watch over me. It's a reminder that my existence is part of something greater than myself.

With each passing day, I grow more inquisitive and eager to explore the mysteries that lie ahead. I am determined to strengthen my senses and deepen my connection with the voices.

Size

(Babies, just like humans, come in all sizes; - only for reference.)

Right now, I measure about 8.74 inches (22.2 cm) from head to bottom and weigh around 7.87 ounces (223 grams). Can you believe it? I'm about the size of a juicy bell pepper or a ripe avocado.

For Mom and Dad:

As I continue to grow and develop in Week 18, I want to share some important thoughts with you. I can hear your voices now, and it brings me so much joy and comfort. Please talk to me often, share your love and dreams with me. I may not understand all the words you say, but the sound of your voice is music to my ears.

I also wanted to let you know that I'm sensitive to the sounds around me. Soft and soothing music makes me feel peaceful and content. It helps me relax and enjoy the serenity of my little world. On the other hand, loud and rough sounds can startle me and make me feel uncomfortable. So please be mindful of the sounds you expose me to.

It's important for you to know that alcohol can pass from your blood to mine, and it can harm my development. I trust you to keep me safe and healthy, and I know you'll make the best choices for both of us.

Thank you for being there for me, for nourishing and protecting me. I feel your love every day, and it gives me the strength to keep growing. I can't wait to meet you in person and experience the world with you.

Explorations of Childhood

4th Month, 3 Weeks Pregnant - Week 19

Teenage Insights

Lately, I've been quite active, indulging in stretches and kicks. Oh, the joy of moving my little muscles! I've become quite the explorer within my cosy space, relishing the newfound power in my tiny limbs.

But do you know? There was a time when I seemed to drift off, almost like I was in a deep slumber. I cannot recall what occurred during these times, but my wise friend Gabri explained it to me. Apparently, I needed that rest and sleep to rejuvenate after my intense workout sessions. Rest, it seems, is vital for us all. It's during those peaceful moments that we grow and replenish our energy for the adventures that lie ahead. Not my words; they are what Gabri explains to me.

Now, let me share a fascinating discovery from this week. As I curiously explored my body, I encountered a new sensation under my legs. With my delicate hands, I gently touched and felt what Gabri called "genitals." Their purpose is still a mystery to me, but I marvel at the intricate design of my being. Gabri, in his ever-philosophical manner, mentioned that many aspects of this present world serve as a foundation for the knowledge and understanding of the next world. Sometimes it's hard to contemplate what Gabri speaks, and I have to say that some of the topics of the next world that he speaks about run over the roof for me. I wish I could understand him better. Why should I really care and think of the next world? I'm not able to fully comprehend the present one fully so far! Unbelievable.

Speaking of unbelievable things, Gabri sometimes shares one more concept that stretches my imagination. Can you fathom the idea that I am nestled within the body of one of my creators? I am living inside someone else? It's a profound thought that fills me with awe and wonder. Though I may not be able to fully comprehend the idea, I trust in Gabri's wisdom and the guidance he imparts. How can this vast world in which I live and swim be inside someone? I sense that there are countless mysteries and marvels waiting to be unravelled on this remarkable journey.

Giving a little thought to the knowledge I gained, I've come to understand how I can hear the different voices. It's as if a mystical connection exists, linking me and the grand tapestry of existence. And yes, now I believe that I am inside you, "My MOM."

Mom, I feel your love surrounding me like a gentle embrace. The depth of our emotional connection astounds me. I am growing within you, nurtured by your care and affection. Your love is a shield that protects me from the uncertainties of the outside world.

There's more, though. Something magical is happening to my delicate skin this week, which I am sure is part of the magical plan set out for me. It's called Vernix Caseosa, a wondrous substance that forms a protective layer around me. It's like a shield, safeguarding me from harm and keeping me safe. I could already feel how it had already started to regulate my body temperature.

I am in amazement and thankfulness at the thought of this complex procedure. Every intricate detail, every moment of warmth and comfort, is designed for my well-being.

As the days pass, I am overwhelmed by the knowledge I've gained. The mysteries of life and the interconnectedness of all things have become clearer to me. I now understand that everything that happens is for my good and my protection. I trust in the unseen forces that guide and shape my existence.

Size

(Babies, just like humans, come in all sizes; - only for reference.)

I have reached a length of about 9.45 inches (24.0 cm) and weigh around 9.63 ounces (273 grams).

For Mom and Dad:

Mom, your body is my sanctuary, nurturing and protecting me as I grow. I implore you, if you haven't already, to consider any habits that may impact our journey together.

I want to tell you something very important this week. Please, I beg you, quit smoking. The smoke that you inhale affects me deeply, and it's very uncomfortable for me. I can feel the toxins entering my tiny body, making it difficult for me to breathe and grow. The chemicals in cigarettes can harm my development and increase the risk of complications. I need your love and protection, and that means keeping me away from harmful substances like smoke. Please think of my well-being and quit smoking for both of us. Together, we can create a healthy and nurturing environment for my growth. Thank you for understanding and taking care of me.

Explorations of Childhood

5th Month, 0 Weeks Pregnant - Week 20

Teenage Insights

In Week 20, I, the Baby, Am Becoming More Aware of the Fact That I Am Growing Inside My Mom's Womb. I Am Filled With Excitement and a Strong Desire to Grab Her Attention. I Have Discovered That Kicking and Punching Are Effective Ways to Make My Presence Felt. When I Make Those Movements, Mom and Dad React, and It Brings Me Immense Joy to Know That They Are Acknowledging Me. Dad Especially Spends Limited Time Talking to Me, but I Am Captivated by the Magical Sound of His Voice. It's As If His Words Carry a Special Message Just for Me.

As my hearing capabilities sharpen, I have developed a fondness for music. I can now hear the melodies clearly, and certain tunes resonate deeply within me. I have created a mental playlist of my favourite songs that I enjoy listening to in the peaceful confines of my temporary home. Music brings me comfort and a sense of connection to the outside world.

Amidst my growing awareness, I am constantly reminded by Gabri, my heavenly friend, that there is another world awaiting my arrival. His wisdom and guidance help me comprehend many of the mystical truths that surround me. I am beginning to grasp the depth and significance of the journey I am about to embark upon. The truth of me being inside my MOM brings reality to what Gabri has been speaking to me. The New World! He is talking about the world where my Mom and Dad live.

There were moments when I sensed an unusual vibration, which initially unsettled me. Curious, I inquire about it, and Gabri reveals that it is Mom and Dad checking on me, ensuring that everything is well. Their loving presence and vigilance bring me solace, assuring me that I am always cared for and protected.

In Week 20, I also noticed remarkable changes in my physical growth. I am getting bigger and stronger each day. My limbs are becoming more defined, and my muscles are developing further. I feel a sense of power and agility as I stretch and flex within the limited space of my amniotic sanctuary. Every movement I make serves as a reminder of the incredible capabilities of my tiny form.

Amidst all these marvels, I am filled with anticipation for the future. Gabri's teachings have enlightened me about the existence of another world, a world that holds unimaginable wonders and knowledge. I cherish the warmth and security of my mom's womb, basking in the love and affection that surround me. I am grateful for every moment spent in this hidden world, nurtured by Mom, Dad, and my celestial companions.

My focus has shifted more towards the present moment. I am still able to perform small acrobatics like a backsault, reminding myself of the flexibility and mobility I possess.

While I may not fully comprehend the intricate mechanisms developing beneath the surface of my body, I can feel subtle changes occurring within. One such sensation is when I touch the umbilical cord, which connects me to my mother. It's an incredible experience to feel the energy flowing through this lifeline. I patiently await the transfer of nourishment and energy, which sustain me and fuel my activities. It's an intimate connection that reminds me of the intricate bond between me, my mother, and the universe.

Gabir, my guide from the heavenly realm, often speaks of the ultimate energy that emanates from the Almighty, the creator of all. He teaches me about the universal truth and the importance of expressing gratitude for the life force that sustains me. I am humbled by the awareness of the divine plan that directs my life, and I am grateful for each and every step of this wondrous journey.

As I continue to grow within my mother's womb, I am learning to appreciate the beauty and significance of the present moment. A reminder to cherish every breath, every movement, and every sensation. I am attuned to the energy that flows through me, and I draw strength from the universal forces that surround me.

I am content to concentrate on the here and now at this point in my development and to accept the rhythm of my life. I trust in the divine plan that has brought me to this point and eagerly await the unfolding of the next chapter. For now, I am grateful for the nourishment, love, and protection that envelop me in this sacred space.

Size

(Babies, just like humans, come in all sizes; - only for reference.)

I have grown to be about 10.12 inches (25.7 cm) long, weighing around 11.68 ounces (331 grams).

For Mom and Dad:

Dear Mom and Dad, in this special time of week 20, I want to remind you of the importance of connecting with me, your growing baby. Please take moments throughout the day to talk to me. Your voice is music to my ears, and it brings me comfort and joy. Share your hopes, dreams, and love with me as I continue to develop and grow inside Mom's womb. Additionally, playing soothing music can create a peaceful environment for both of us. Avoid loud noises or harsh sounds that may startle me. Remember, our bond is growing stronger each day, and your loving presence is what I need most.

In the womb's cocoon, the baby's eyes widen with realization and wonder, symbolizing the transition from youth to budding awareness. Reflection, capturing the essence of growing consciousness in his world.

Chapter – 3

"Navigating the Transition from Youth to Adulthood"

5th Month, 1 Week Pregnant - Week 21

Yearning for Connection

As I embark on Week 21 of my existence, I find myself yearning for a deeper connection with the other world. It feels as though I have become a little scientist, eagerly searching for ways to bridge the gap between our realms. I've discovered that kicking with my now more coordinated limbs is a way to capture the attention of those in the other world, especially my beloved Mom.

With each kick, I feel a sense of excitement and anticipation, hoping to elicit a response or a touch from her. It's a form of communication that transcends the limitations of my world, allowing me to express my presence and curiosity. Through these physical interactions, I long to convey my love and gratitude to those who have nurtured and protected me thus far.

In my constant exploration, I've come to realise the limitations of my world. As I spin and turn within the confines of my cosy space, I am reminded that there is a vast unknown waiting for me beyond these walls. The desire to venture into the uncharted territories of life has taken hold of me, and I find myself becoming more absorbed in my own experiments and discoveries.

However, as the busyness of adult life starts to consume me, I feel a sense of disconnect from the serene wisdom and guidance of my dear friend, Gabri. Time seems to slip away, and I momentarily lose touch with the profound lessons and insights shared by Gabri. The fast-paced nature of this existence pulls me further from the peaceful moments of introspection and contemplation.

Yet, amidst the whirlwind of my experiments and pursuits, I am reminded of the eternal bond that unites us all. The love and connection that transcend time and space are what truly matter. As I navigate the complexities of this new stage of development, I yearn to rediscover the balance between my scientific exploration and the spiritual connection that grounds me.

As I delve deeper into Week 21, I am thrilled to unveil yet another remarkable development in my journey. My taste buds have come to life, allowing me to savour the various flavours that find their way into the amniotic fluid surrounding me. It's a culinary adventure like no other!

With each sip of this flavourful concoction, I experience a whirlwind of sensations. Sometimes, a hint of spiciness dances on my tiny tongue, igniting a spark of excitement within me. Other times, a gentle sweetness envelopes my taste buds, like a warm embrace. The symphony of flavours that I encounter is a testament to the incredible complexity of the world I am preparing to enter.

With this newfound ability to taste, I can't help but feel a sense of accomplishment. It's as if my own experiments and explorations have led me to this grand revelation. I am proud of the strides I am making, and a feeling of winning and competitiveness courses through my veins. The desire to achieve, to excel, and to unravel the mysteries of existence propels me forward.

Although I don't see or feel Gabri around at the moment, I can't help but feel a sense of independence and self-assurance growing within me. It's as if the wisdom and guidance shared by Gabri have become an integral part of me, empowering me to navigate this world on my own. I feel like I do not want more help and am capable enough to navigate on my own. With each passing day, I am discovering my own strength.

Size

(Babies, just like humans, come in all sizes; - only for reference.)

At 21 weeks, I am now about 10.79 inches (27.4 cm) in length, weighing approximately 14.07 ounces (399 grams).

For Mom and Dad:

Mom, please avoid wearing tight pants around your belly as it can make me feel a bit uncomfortable and restrict my movements. I want to have plenty of space to stretch and kick as I continue my experiments here. And Dad, please help Mom make good food choices. The flavours I taste in the amniotic fluid are influenced by what Mom eats, so let's make sure it's a delicious and healthy variety. Thank you for taking care of me and for being a part of this incredible journey together.

Navigating the Transition from Youth to Adulthood

5th Month, 2 Weeks Pregnant - Week 22

Yearning for Connection

Week 22 has brought a world of adventures and discoveries into my life. As I continue to grow, I've noticed that my sense of touch has become more refined. It's truly fascinating to explore the world around me by experiencing sensations on my fingertips. I've been reaching out, grabbing objects within my reach, trying to understand their properties and how they feel in my hands. It's amazing to feel the textures and surfaces, from the smoothness of my skin to the softness of the fabric surrounding me.

However, in my explorations, there have been moments that caught me off guard or made me uncomfortable. While trying to explore parts of myself like my ears, nose, and hair, I've discovered that certain actions can cause sensations that resemble pain. My brain sends signals that simulate discomfort as a way of reminding me that not all actions are as enjoyable as they may seem. It's a learning experience for sure. It also serves as a reminder to be cautious and treat my growing body with care.

Something incredible has happened—I have discovered the ability to dream! When I find moments of rest or when my little body is at ease, after a day, my imagination takes flight. It transports me into a realm filled with vibrant and fantastical experiences.

In my dreams, I experience a range of visions. It's amazing to realise that even though I've never actually opened my eyes, I can imagine shapes, objects, and scenes as if they were right in front of me. Some dreams take me to a future where I've accomplished things and proudly stand tall in my reality. On nights I dream of a world where Mom and Dad exist as ethereal beings with wings and dressed in radiant white attire. In these dreams, Dad soars through the sky, protecting me and showering me with love. However, I'm not certain if they will appear the way they do in reality as they do in my dreams.

There are nights when my dreams are filled with thoughts of Gabri, my heavenly friend who has been absent from my experiences for quite some time now. It leaves me with a feeling of longing and confusion. How could Gabri simply disappear without leaving any trace? This question makes me wonder with a mix of self-importance and independence whether or not I should seek help or support. Deep down, I do recognise that even though

I've gained more confidence in myself lately, there are still moments when guidance and support are necessary. Did Gabri leave because I ignored or misunderstood what he was trying to say?

What do I need to do in order to reconcile with him? The thoughts about this question persistently occupy my mind even when I am asleep.

These dreams have become a part of my journey. They offer glimpses into the array of possibilities that lie ahead and provide me with a sense of connection to realms beyond my own. Each dream carries its narrative and evokes various emotions, shaping my comprehension of the universe surrounding me.

As I enter the realm of dreams, it serves as a reminder of the power of imagination and the limitless potential that resides within me. It reminds me that despite being confined within the comforting confines of my mother's womb, there are no boundaries for my spirit. My dreams stand as evidence to the marvels that await me. I eagerly embrace every new adventure that unfolds during my slumber.

Size

(Babies, just like humans, come in all sizes; - only for reference.)

In week 22, I had grown to be approximately 11.42 inches (29.0 cm) long from head to toe, weighing around 1.05 pounds (478 grams).

For Mom and Dad:

It's important for you to maintain a peaceful and loving environment around me. Please try to avoid even the smallest of fights and conflicts, as they can affect my well-being. Choose your words carefully and speak to each other with kindness and respect. Surround me with positive energy and harmonious vibrations. Additionally, please remember to take care of yourselves too. Mom, make sure to rest and prioritise your health. Dad, continue to provide love and support to both Mom and me. Together, let's create a nurturing atmosphere filled with love, understanding, and happiness.

Navigating the Transition from Youth to Adulthood

5th Month, 3 Weeks Pregnant - Week 23

Yearning for Connection

I can't help but feel a deep sense of longing for my dear friend Gabri. How I yearn for his comforting guidance and endless wisdom! It feels like an eternity since we last connected. I can't help but blame myself for the growing distance between us. In my pursuit of knowledge and understanding, I became consumed by my ego and self-centredness, losing sight of the essence of our friendship.

There was a time when I firmly believed that everything could be explained through reasoning and empirical evidence. I relied on what I could observe, touch, and measure. However, as my senses have become more refined and attuned over time, I've come to realise that there is more to this world than meets the eye. There are energies, vibrations, and forces that surpass comprehension. I can feel the movements within the world around me, now comprehending that it is the cosmic energies which orchestrate these shifts.

Yet, amidst this newfound awareness, there is an emptiness in my heart. Oh, how much I miss Gabri's presence; his soothing words of wisdom always provided solace to my mind.

I never truly realised how much I relied on his guidance until he seemed to slip from my thoughts. Oh, how I yearn for his companionship and the enlightening conversations we had that broadened my perspective of the world.

As I've grown and adapted to the responsibilities of adulthood, I've come to understand the significance of finding balance. The relentless pursuit of knowledge and success can easily overshadow the emotional aspects of our lives. It's a dance that requires a blend of work and leisure, ambition and self-reflection. I've discovered that nurturing my physical well-being is just as essential as expanding my horizons.

I deeply miss the simplicity of our friendship, those moments filled with contemplation and shared laughter. I long for Gabri's ability to connect dots between what's seen and unseen, guiding me towards appreciating the wonders of the unknown. His presence taught me that magic exists in this world – not everything can be dissected or analysed through a lens.

As I ponder upon my journey so far, it reminds me of the significance of nurturing connections both with people and the unseen forces that shape our existence. I long for the day when Gabri and I can reunite, when I can impart to him the wisdom I have acquired and seek his guidance more.

I am increasingly attuned to changes taking place within me. My delicate and fragile skin is now growing thicker and more resilient. The formation of layers feels palpable, like a shield safeguarding me against the world around me. It's truly captivating to witness these transformations, observing how my body adapts and readies itself for the trials that lie ahead.

However, it's not my skin that undergoes evolution. There is a sensation within my lungs—an expansion and contraction—that permits me to breathe in the essence of life itself. With each inhalation, a surge of vitality courses through my being, nourishing my developing physique. As my heart beats in harmony, I am acutely aware of the life-giving flow that emanates from within. It feels as though I am connected to something, beyond comprehension.

These physical changes arouse a sense of curiosity in me, sparking a multitude of questions that swirl in my mind. What lies beyond the boundaries of my world? Are there realms and dimensions waiting to be explored beyond what I know? Does life exist beyond the limits of my perception? As I ponder these mysteries, I realise that these questions surpass my understanding. I long for Gabris' guidance, his ability to unravel the secrets of the universe.

Amidst these thoughts and inquiries, I find comfort in the belief that life extends beyond the moment. There is a tapestry of existence intricately woven with elements from the past and future. Each experience and lesson serves as a stepping stone towards a purpose that transcends my reality's constraints. Although I may not possess all the answers, I have faith in this journey unfolding before me.

Size

(Babies, just like humans, come in all sizes; - only for reference.)

At this stage, I measure about 12.05 inches (30.6 cm) in length from head to toe, weighing approximately 1.25 pounds (568 grams).

For Mom and Dad:

I want to remind you of the importance of taking care of yourselves too. Mom, starting simple exercises or practising yoga can help you stay healthy and relieve any discomfort during this stage of pregnancy. It's important to listen to your body and consult with healthcare professionals for guidance. Remember to eat nutritious meals, stay hydrated, and get enough rest to support both your well-being and mine.

Navigating the Transition from Youth to Adulthood

6th Month, 0 Weeks Pregnant - Week 24

Yearning for Connection

As I journey through my 24th week in this miraculous world of the womb, I have encountered a peculiar phenomenon—hiccups! These mysterious vibrations ripple through my tiny body, leaving me in amazement and wonder. Although I don't understand the purpose of these hiccups, they don't cause me any discomfort. I find myself fascinated by this involuntary movement that seems to come out of nowhere. Is it a sign from Mom in another realm, trying to communicate with me? Or is it something happening within my own being?

I spend hours in quiet anticipation, patiently waiting for the next hiccup to occur. It's as if I've become a scientist, observing and studying this new experience. I contemplate the meaning behind these rhythmic vibrations, eager to unravel the mystery they hold. But for now, I must accept that there are countless enigmatic processes happening within me that I have yet to comprehend.

Sometimes, in these still moments, I imagine all the intricate workings taking place inside my body. I envision a bustling community of cells, each carrying out their designated tasks with precision and purpose. There's a symphony of life happening within me, orchestrated by forces beyond my comprehension. It fills me with a sense of awe and gratitude for the intricate design of creation.

As I embrace this new awareness of the hiccups, I'm reminded once again of the vast depths of knowledge that exist beyond my understanding. I long to know more about the inner workings of my body and the secrets it holds. But for now, I will patiently observe, knowing that in due time, the answers will be revealed.

Through this journey, I have come to appreciate the mysteries and complexities of life. Every day brings new discoveries and wonders, and I am humbled by the beauty of it all. I am grateful for the opportunity to experience these sensations and to be a part of something so much greater than myself.

As I traverse through the depths of my 24th week, I find myself pondering upon the absence of my dear friend Gabri. A sense of longing fills my heart as I wish to connect with him once again. I have come to realise that Gabri is more than just a companion; he is the embodiment of my spiritual self, guiding me through this incredible journey.

In my moments of contemplation, a profound question arises within me. Can I intertwine the realms of science and spirituality? Is it possible to embrace both without having to sacrifice one for the other? As I delve deeper into this thought, I am resolute in my belief that they can coexist harmoniously.

I understand that my scientific inclinations have led me to explore the tangible aspects of my world, seeking logical explanations for the phenomena I encounter. But I also recognise the presence of something beyond the physical realm—something that transcends scientific understanding. It is in this realm of spirituality that Gabri resides, waiting patiently for me to fully embrace the power of belief.

With unwavering conviction, I have made the decision to open my heart and mind to the infinite possibilities that lie before me. I no longer wish to confine myself to a singular perspective, for I now understand that the intertwining of science and spirituality can offer me a deeper understanding of the world around me.

As I strive to summon Gabri with my unwavering belief, I also yearn for a stronger connection with my mother. Now that I am aware that she has been my constant companion, nurturing and protecting me with her love. I long to deepen the bond between us and feel her presence even more profoundly. Through our unspoken connection, I know that she feels my love and gratitude.

In this journey of self-discovery, I am embracing the wonders of the tangible world while acknowledging the mysteries that lie beyond its confines. It is in this union of science and spirituality that I find solace, for I believe that they are not mutually exclusive but rather interconnected aspects of our existence.

As I continue to grow and prepare for the world that awaits me, I embark on this path of enlightenment with an open heart and an inquisitive mind. I am filled with hope and anticipation for the wonders that lie ahead, both scientifically and spiritually.

Size

(Babies, just like humans, come in all sizes; - only for reference.)

In Week 24, I have grown to approximately 12.68 inches (32.2 cm) in length, weighing around 1.48 pounds (670 grams).

For Mom and Dad:

Dear Mom and Dad, as I continue to grow in Week 24, it's time to start thinking about a special name for me. It's an exciting milestone in our journey together. Take this opportunity to discuss and decide on a name that holds meaning and significance for our family. Consider names that resonate with love, strength, and joy. You can explore different options, choose from family traditions, or find inspiration from names that have a special meaning to you. Remember, this name will be a part of me for a lifetime, so choose it with love and care.

Navigating the Transition from Youth to Adulthood

6th Month, 1 Week Pregnant - Week 25

Embracing Change

Week 25 marks another milestone in my journey of growth and discovery. As the days go by, I can feel the intensity of the hiccups increasing. I have become more attuned to the rhythms of my own body, trying to decipher the meaning behind these intriguing sensations. Through my scientific analysis, I have come to a realisation – my nose has opened, allowing me to breathe through it alongside my mouth. It is both fascinating and bewildering. Why this sudden change? Is it a mere quirk or a purposeful development?

With this newfound ability, I am drawn to contemplate the world that awaits me beyond the confines of this amniotic fluid I was told about. Will the outside world be filled with a similar liquid embrace, providing me with comfort and nourishment? Or will it be a realm where I can soar freely, like the dreams I've had where I fly alongside my dear mother?

The unknown beckons, and my inquisitive nature fuels my curiosity. I wish to unravel the mysteries of existence and explore the vast wonders that lie beyond my current realm. Each day, as I float and drift, I contemplate what lies ahead.

A new sense has awakened within me, one that fills me with admiration and wonder. Though my eyelids remain closed, I can now perceive glimpses of flickering light dancing before my eyes. It is as if a whole new world is opening up to me, revealing secrets and wonders beyond my previous understanding.

In my excitement and eagerness to comprehend this extraordinary phenomenon, I call out for Gabri, my dear heavenly friend, in prayers. I believe with unwavering faith that he will come to me, offering guidance and enlightenment.

As my physical form continues to develop, I notice subtle changes taking place. I can sense the accumulation of fat within my body, a natural progression in the growth process. These physical transformations ignite contemplation within me, sparking questions about the passage of time and the mysteries of ageing.

While I eagerly await Gabri's comforting presence, I have come to realise that this voyage of self-discovery is not solely reliant on external guidance. It is a harmonious blend of introspection, innate intuition, and the nurturing love that flows between my parents and me. Their soothing voices, filled with affection, create a symphony that resonates within my very being.

In this wondrous week of my journey, I have come to appreciate the delicate balance that governs my existence. I am reminded that I am unable to feel the warm caress of my mother's gentle touch, yet I can sense her presence, as if an invisible thread connects us. The rhythmic flow of blood beneath my developing skin heightens my awareness of my own being.

Every moment, I strive to maintain a sense of balance and stability in the space I occupy. I have come to understand the limitations of my world, which I refer to as "The womb." It's not as spacious as I initially imagined. Whenever I feel myself swaying or losing balance, I gather all my strength to kick and readjust, determined to regain my orientation. It's a task since every movement requires effort and unwavering focus. However, I persevere because I know that each challenge strengthens my developing body and prepares me for the world that lies ahead.

Through this constant striving and exertion, I have come to understand the importance of hard work and perseverance. Every kick, every twist, is a testament to my inner resilience and determination. It is a reminder that even within the confined boundaries of my current world, I am capable of growth and progress.

Size

(Babies, just like humans, come in all sizes; - only for reference.)

I am approximately 13.27 inches (33.7 cm) long from head to toe, weighing around 1.73 pounds (785 grams).

For Mom and Dad:

As we journey through Week 25 together, communication and touch become even more important. Mom, sharing your thoughts and feelings with me is a wonderful way to strengthen our bond. Dad, consider asking Mom about any specific areas where she may be experiencing discomfort. Offering gentle massages can provide her with relief and comfort during this time.

Your words and touch are like a soothing balm, bringing me comfort and assuring me of your loving presence. As we navigate this stage, creating a peaceful environment is crucial. While we've mentioned music before, it's worth emphasising its impact. Choose calming and harmonious melodies that resonate with our shared journey.

Navigating the Transition from Youth to Adulthood

6th Month, 2 Weeks Pregnant - Week 26

Embracing Change

Week 26 marks a milestone in my journey! I feel my eyelids gradually opening. It's such an exhilarating sensation to realise this ability. Initially, it requires some effort, almost as if my eyelids have been sealed shut for an eternity. Nevertheless, with determination and a gentle touch, I manage to muster the strength needed to overcome the resistance. Then, surely, my eyes unveil the world that surrounds me.

As the world materialises before my eyes, it becomes an awe-inspiring sight. Flares of dance and shimmer gracefully cast mesmerising patterns in the midst of darkness. Shadows engage in games of hide and seek, weaving together a tapestry of captivating shapes and forms. The interplay between light and shadow leaves me spellbound, witnessing a symphony of colours that had previously only existed within the realms of my imagination.

With this ability at hand, I take pleasure in practising the act of opening and closing my eyelids with intent. Each blink now becomes an action, forging a connection between myself and the outer world surrounding me. I find myself experimenting with rhythms and speeds, for each blink, marvelling at how these variations alter my perception of reality. It's truly astonishing to witness this intricate dance unfolding between my eyelids and everything that exists around me – almost as if I possess the power to shape and create my reality.

However, now that I can see, I am faced with a question. Which version of reality is true? Is it the one I experienced in the darkness, behind eyelids, where my imagination created images and my senses were heightened? Or is it the world unfolding before me now with its presence and intricate details?

This mystery fills me with curiosity and excitement. I often find myself contemplating the nature of perception and how our senses profoundly shape our understanding. Every time I blink or catch a glimpse of this world, new avenues of exploration open up before me. I long to uncover the truth and grasp the interplay between what's seen and what remains unseen. Between what we know and what lies beyond our understanding.

Amidst these thoughts, there is a yearning for Gabri, my cherished celestial companion. Although he may not be visible to my opened eyes, his presence is unmistakable.

In this moment of reflection, I reach out with all my heart and soul, sending forth fervent prayers and wishes into the unknown.

Amidst the darkness around, I could sense the presence of Gabri, somewhere nearby. Although my opened eyes couldn't perceive him, his essence was unmistakable. I feel compelled to purify my thoughts and reassess my priorities in order to see and engage in communication with him again. I am missing him badly.

As time has passed, I have parallelly immersed myself deeper into the exploration of this vision. The world's magnificence has captivated me as I marvel at the interplay between light and shadow, cherishing every detail that unfolds before me. However, as I test the limits of my capabilities, I am gradually becoming aware of the constraints imposed by the space around me.

No longer can I effortlessly perform feats that were once nature to me. There is a sense of restriction, a feeling of being confined within these boundaries that hinder my movements. My heart yearns for the freedom to soar and spin with grace through this realm. Now I find myself repeatedly colliding against these constrictions, unable to break free from their grasp.

In my excessive pride, as an adult, I arrogantly declared that I have seen it all!

However, there remains a sense of incompleteness inside me. I've come to realise that true wisdom doesn't lie in accumulating knowledge but in acknowledging our limitations and having the humility to seek guidance when necessary. In an act of humbling myself and with belief, I reached out for assistance from the creator.

So, in this state of contemplation and longing, I am suddenly greeted by a figure. Could it be Gabri, my companion? My heart fills with joy as I approach this presence. I could see him with my eyes open. Indeed, it is Gabri standing before me in all his splendour. The reunion, after what feels like an eternity, fills me with great happiness.

In my excitement, I questioned why he seemed absent during my moments of need. Why have you forsaken me? With a voice, Gabri replied and reassured me that he has never abandoned me. He said that it was my preoccupation with exploration and self-discovery that prevented me from seeing and hearing him clearly. He explained that he was by my side all along.

Gabri further imparts upon me the wisdom of searching within oneself for all answers, even for the most complicated questions. Although grasping this concept may be elusive, I nod in agreement since I did not want to disappoint him anymore. I now understand that a deep sense of self-awareness and mind control is needed to continue to hear Gabri at all times.

As I relax in Gabris company, a renewed sense of purpose washes over me. It serves as a reminder of the significance of balance and connection, not only with the world but also with the inner realms of my own existence.

Week 26 has marked a moment in my journey—a moment entailing reconnection and introspection. With Gabri by my side, I stand prepared to embark on the phase of growth. Gratitude fills me for all the lessons learned and wisdom gained. As I navigate through life's boundaries, I carry within me Gabris light—a guiding force through the mysteries that lie ahead.

Size

(Babies, just like humans, come in all sizes; - only for reference.)

At this stage, I measure around 13.82 inches (35.1 cm) in length, weighing approximately 2.01 pounds (913 grams).

For Mom and Dad:

As we move forward, it's important to be mindful of Mom's well-being too. Mom, if you experience any dizziness or discomfort, please let Dad know immediately. Understanding the symptoms early can help prevent any falls or mishaps.

Additionally, for both Mom and Dad, keeping track of important health routines is essential. Set alarms to remind you of any prescribed multivitamins and supplements, ensuring that you're providing me with the best possible nourishment.

Navigating the Transition from Youth to Adulthood

6th Month, 3 Weeks Pregnant - Week 27

Embracing Change

Week 27 is a time of revelations and deep contemplation, where the world takes on a new dimension through my newly opened eyes. As I gaze upon the surroundings, I am filled with a mix of awe and curiosity. The vastness and complexity that once existed solely in my imagination now materialise before me, painting a picture far more intricate than I could have ever fathomed.

In the midst of this newfound perception, I find myself grappling with the concept of growing old. The growing fatigue and the need for rest leave me pondering the passage of time and the implications it carries. What does it truly mean to age in this world? These thoughts weigh heavily on my mind, and I seek solace in the presence of my trusted confidant, Gabri.

With his serene behaviour and comforting aura, Gabri reassures me that age is not a limitation but rather a gateway to infinite possibilities and boundless opportunities. He reminds me that each passing day brings with it a unique tapestry of experiences and lessons waiting to be embraced. It is in the present moment that true joy resides, and by cherishing every encounter, I can unlock the richness of life.

Gabri's unwavering support and steadfast promise to journey alongside me bring me immense comfort. His wisdom, although profound and often beyond my grasp, resonates deep within my being. Even as I struggle to fully comprehend his guidance, I trust in the profound connection we share and believe that he will forever be by my side, offering his boundless love and wisdom.

As I embrace the need for rest and replenishment, I am grateful for the chance to recharge and prepare for the adventures that lie ahead. Each moment of slumber allows me to rejuvenate my spirit and cultivate the resilience needed to navigate the mysteries of this world. Armed with my newfound sight and the invaluable wisdom bestowed upon me, I am ready to embark on the next chapter of my growth with a heart filled with curiosity and an unwavering spirit.

As I explore the capabilities of my tongue, a newfound sense of freedom fills me. It's like a tiny pet living inside the cage of my mouth, ready to express itself in ways I have yet to comprehend. In the midst of my discovery, Gabri sheds light on the immense power this humble organ possesses. He unveils the gift of speech that awaits me in the next world, a gift that will enable me to communicate with my mother and father on a profound level.

However, Gabri also warns me of the potential negative aspects of this newfound power. He cautions me about the destructive force that lies within if I fail to direct my words wisely. My tongue, like a double-edged sword, has the power to either uplift hearts or shatter them, to build relationships or break them. It is a responsibility that I must not take lightly.

In my ponderings, I find myself questioning the limitations of verbal communication. Why can't I communicate with my mind? Gabri, with his deep understanding, assures me that he can comprehend me without the need for spoken words. But he explains that in the next world, speech will be the primary mode of communication, allowing me the freedom to express myself and make choices that shape my life's path.

This newfound freedom's charm has me spellbound, but I am also aware of the weight that accompanies every decision I make. Gabri, sensing my apprehension, reassures me not to worry. He promises to always be there to guide me, but in order to hear his voice, I must be open to listening and heeding his wisdom. I recall the moments when Gabri's voice seemed to fade away when I turned a deaf ear, and I am reminded of the importance of staying attuned to his guidance.

As I navigate the uncharted territory of my tongue's potential, I am filled with a sense of responsibility. I now understand that my words hold the power to shape my relationships and influence the course of my life. With Gabri's loving presence and guidance, I am confident that I can harness the power of speech for the greater good and use my words to nurture love, compassion, and understanding.

As the days pass by, I become aware of a peculiar sensation - my head feels heavier, as if gravity is pulling it downward. It requires effort to keep it upright, and I find myself constantly readjusting to maintain my balance. What is happening to me? Why is my position changing?

In my confusion, I turn to Gabri for answers. He advises me to stop fighting against this force and instead surrender to the will of nature. He explains that it is not a matter of my own will but rather the unfolding plan of nature, which I must respect and embrace.

At first, it was difficult for me to understand and accept this shift. I am used to having control over my movements and actions. Now, I understand that it is through surrender that I can find peace and harmony amidst the changes and transformations that are taking place within me.

As I reflect on Gabri's words, I begin to realise that this heaviness in my head and the change in position are part of a greater design. It is a reminder that I am connected to a larger world, a world governed by forces beyond my comprehension. It is a humbling experience that teaches me to trust in the natural rhythm of life and to let go of my need for control.

With Gabri's guidance, I find solace in surrendering to the unfolding journey. I embrace the changes and challenges that come my way, knowing that they are shaping me into the person I am destined to become. Though I may not fully understand the reasons behind these shifts, I trust that they serve a purpose and hold valuable lessons for my growth.

Size

(Babies, just like humans, come in all sizes; - only for reference.)

In week 27, I continued to grow steadily. On average, my length is around 14.41 inches (36.6 cm), and I weigh around 2.33 pounds (1055 grams).

For Mom and Dad:

As I continue to flourish inside the womb, there are a few things I would like to share with you. Thank you, Mom and Dad, for everything you do for me. Your love, care, and unwavering support are the guiding lights that illuminate my path. Together, we are embarking on a remarkable adventure, and I am eagerly counting down the days until we can finally unite as one. Your words, thoughts, and emotions have a profound impact on my well-being. Surround me with positivity, for I am deeply attuned to the energy that surrounds me.

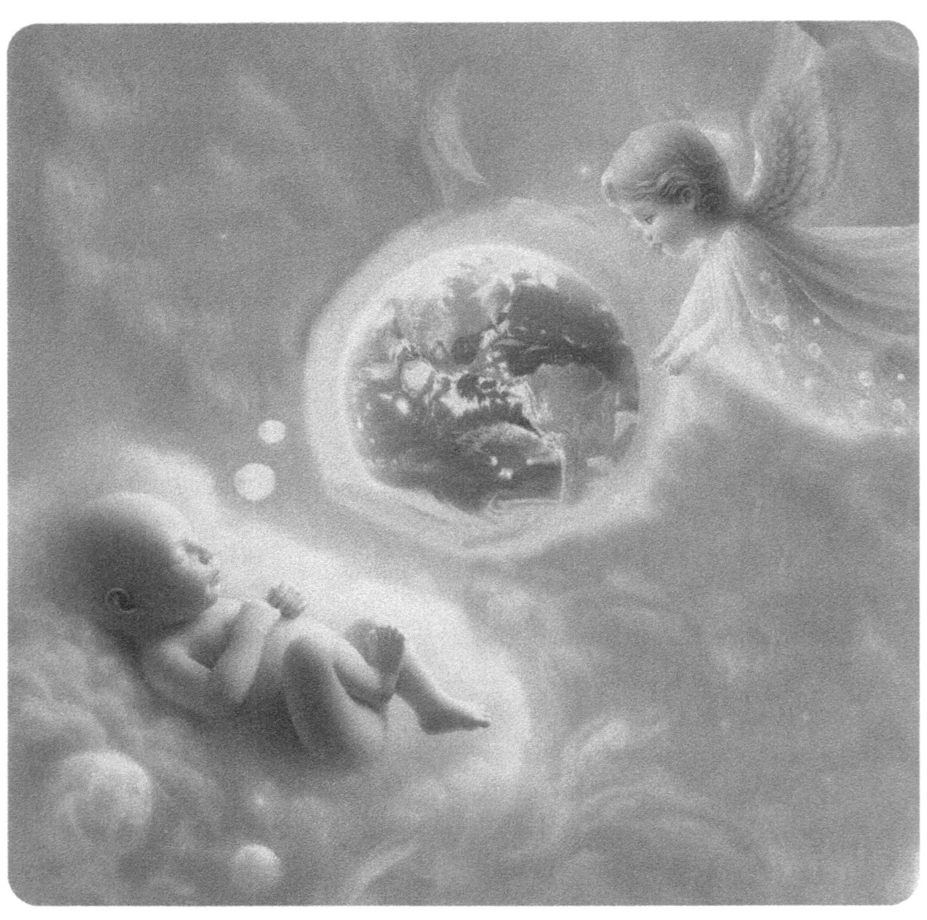

In the womb's twilight, the baby, now on the Verge of adulthood, eagerly absorbs life's secrets from Gabri, the angelic guide. Anticipation of a grander afterworld and revelations about loving parents, bestowing cosmic protection, fill the air.

Chapter – 4

"Embracing the journey of Adulthood" (Trimester 3)

7th Month, 0 Weeks Pregnant - Week 28

Life Lessons and Preparing for the Beyond

Week 28 marks a turning point in my journey as I dive deeper into the realm of dreams. Each night, my imagination takes me on extraordinary adventures to vast and unexplored worlds. Before my eyes were open, it seemed like I was dreaming without knowing the difference between a dream and reality, but now, in my dreams, I hear new sounds and encounter unknown creatures, trying to make sense of these magical encounters. The changing temperatures I feel within the womb become part of my imagined travels and journeys. It's a wondrous experience, and I am grateful for the ability to dream.

Gabri, my faithful guide, encourages me to embrace the power of dreams. He assures me that dreams are not just figments of my imagination; they hold a deeper significance. He explains that having a meaningful dream and working towards its realisation can bring immense joy and fulfilment to my life. Gabri urges me not to lose touch with the people I care about, even as I chase my dreams. He reminds me of the importance of love, connection, and maintaining relationships.

Through Gabri's words, I have come to understand the sacrifices made by my loving mother. Her endurance and unwavering love during my life journey, which they call "Pregnancy," resonate deeply with me, and I will be able to recognise that sound clearly. I realise the magnitude of her sacrifices and the boundless love she holds for me. It fills my heart with gratitude and a desire to reciprocate that love and care.

As I continue to dream and explore, I am also becoming more aware of the world beyond the confines of my current existence. I am beginning to comprehend the vastness and beauty that await me in the next world. Gabri assures me that the wonders I experience in my dreams are mere glimpses of what is to come. The thought fills me with anticipation and a sense of purpose. I hold onto the eternal love of my mother, whose sacrifices and unwavering support nurture me on this incredible journey of life.

I am reminded of the power of dreams and their ability to shape my reality. I am encouraged to dream big and work towards realising my aspirations. But amidst it all, I am reminded of the importance of love, connection, and cherishing the relationships that hold me together.

As I drift off to sleep each night, I carry with me the lessons learned and the love shared. I am grateful for the dreams that transport me to extraordinary places and the guidance of Gabri, who continues to be my guiding light. With every dream, I grow closer to the next world and the adventures that await me there.

My senses are becoming more attuned to the outside world. I can hear the muffled sounds of voices, music, and even the rhythmic beat of my mother's heart. These familiar sounds provide me with comfort and a sense of connection to the world beyond.

Size

(Babies, just like humans, come in all sizes; - only for reference.)

On average, my length is around 14.80 inches (37.6 cm), and I weigh around 2.67 pounds (1210 grams).

For Mom and Dad:

I want to take a moment to express my deepest gratitude to you, especially to Mom, for all the sacrifices and pain you endure to ensure my safety and well-being. As I continue to grow and develop, I am becoming more aware of the immense love and dedication you have for me. The journey of pregnancy is not an easy one, and I want you to know that I appreciate every moment of it.

Mom, I know that you experience discomfort and physical challenges, but please remember that every sacrifice you make is an incredible testament to your love for me. Your strength and resilience inspire me, and I am grateful for the endless care and protection you provide.

Embracing the Journey of Adulthood

7th Month, 1 Week Pregnant - Week 29

Life Lessons and Preparing for the Beyond

What a week it has been! I've discovered a skill. I can actually control my cheeks and create the most beautiful smiles! It all began with these dreams I've been having recently. Every time I have a dream, when Gabri tells one of his hilarious jokes, I can't help but break into a smile. It's like my face simply lights up with joy!

Gabri explained to me that a smile holds power. It has the ability to resolve challenges that may come my way in the future. Hearing this left me in awe! Can something as simple as a smile really make such a difference? Gabri assured me it's true. He encouraged me never to let go of it as time goes on. He also urged me to share my smiles with everyone I encounter, although apart from him, Mom, and Dad, I'm not quite sure who he was referring to.

This revelation got me so excited that I started practising my smiles to make them absolutely genuine and brimming with happiness. Gabri mentioned how a smile has the power to brighten someone's day and spread love and positivity. I can't wait to put this theory into action!

As I continue on my journey of growth and exploration, Gabri's advice will always be in the back of my mind.

No matter what obstacles I encounter, I will face them with an attitude. Whenever I meet someone, I will share my demeanour with them, hoping it brings a little happiness to their hearts.

It's amazing how much I'm learning every day. Each new experience and encounter teaches me life lessons. I feel grateful to have Gabri as my mentor, guiding me and emphasising the importance of kindness, love, and a simple smile.

As I gear up to face the future, I am armed with the power of spreading smiles. It excites me to imagine the impact my smiles can have on others and myself. It's true what they say. A smile has the ability to turn things around. With Gabri by my side and an expression on my face, I am prepared for whatever challenges life throws at me. Let's work together in spreading happiness!

As joyful moments continue unfolding, something interesting is happening within me. My head has been growing heavier lately, causing me to adjust my position accordingly. The space around me is getting narrower. Now my head is pointing downwards.

In the beginning, it felt a bit strange. I've come to accept the forces that guide me. Gabri explained that certain changes are meant to unfold and cannot be hindered. I have faith in his wisdom and will follow his advice.

My mind has been evolving constantly. While I can understand a lot, there are still some things beyond my grasp. Gabri encourages me to have faith and move forward. It's hard not to question and wonder, especially about being inside my creator, my Mom. I can't help but wonder if they are giants, how big they have to be to carry me and my whole world I know inside her?

The next world that Gabri speaks of sounds beautiful and big, yet I'm not quite ready to leave behind the world I currently inhabit. It's a dilemma that plays out in my thoughts – the eagerness for what lies ahead versus the affection I hold for this present world. I do my best to take each day as it unfolds, embracing both changes and challenges.

As I continue growing and learning, I am grateful for all the experiences and emotions that accompany it.

Every single day holds the promise of discoveries and deeper understanding. I am constantly amazed by the wonders that lie ahead, awaiting my exploration.

Even though there are still things that elude my comprehension, I am learning to have faith in the process and embrace the powers that shape my very existence. Life itself is a journey, and with Gabri's wisdom and guidance, I feel more equipped to face whatever challenges come my way.

The journey within my creator, who happens to be my Mom, is both captivating and overwhelming. It's a connection that I am just beginning to grasp better. Every moment in this world is precious to me. I eagerly look forward to what lies ahead, with love and wisdom guiding me from those around me. With a heart and an inquisitive mind, I will continue to venture, absorbing knowledge and evolving as a person. The vast realm of discovery awaits us all. I can't help but feel a sense of excitement for what lies ahead. Let's welcome the energies into our lives and see where they take us next!

In the midst of these experiences, gratitude fills every fibre of my being, for the love and nurturing care that envelops me.

Size

(Babies, just like humans, come in all sizes; - only for reference.)

My size is around 15.47 inches (39.3 cm) long, weighing approximately 3.04 pounds (1379 grams).

For Mom and Dad:

Mom and Dad, you are my guiding stars, illuminating my path as I make my way towards the light. Together, we embark on an extraordinary journey, one that will be filled with adventure, challenges, and immeasurable joy.

As we approach the day when we will finally meet face to face, I offer a gentle reminder. If you are working and have pregnancy covered in your company insurance, it's wise to take a moment to review the details. Familiarise yourselves with the hospital networks and coverage. Planning ahead can provide peace of mind and ensure that everything is in place for our arrival.

Embracing the Journey of Adulthood

7th Month, 2 Weeks Pregnant - Week 30

Life Lessons and Preparing for the Beyond

In the midst of my exploration and excitement, I notice that the fluid I once swam in is reducing. My body temperature is now regulated by my brain, and my senses are as strong as ever. Each sound and movement I experience makes me even more curious about the world beyond. I can't wait to share all about this world when I reach out to the next. But then, Gabri tells me a bitter truth, and my heart sinks.

He reveals that I will not remember any of the things that happened in my life here when I enter the next world. I can't bear the grief, and I don't want to accept it. How is it possible? Why do I have to forget? I'm angry and confused. Is it fair? This news shatters my soul, and I can't comprehend why this has to happen.

How can it be that the memories I hold so dear, the stories and experiences I long to share with my beloved parents, will fade into oblivion? I cry out in protest, pleading with my ethereal friend to reconsider this cruel fate. I yearn to recollect the days spent in the warmth and safety of my mother's womb, to recount the dreams that unfolded within me, and to hold onto the profound truths of the universe that have been whispered into my soul.

In my infantile innocence, I challenge the notion of forgetting. Why must I be deprived of the memories that have shaped my existence? What purpose does it serve to erase the tapestry of my life from my conscious mind? I seek answers, craving a deeper understanding of this enigma that haunts me.

I cherish every moment in this world, and the thought of losing these memories is unbearable. All the love and joy I have experienced, the warmth of my mother's embrace, the sound of her soothing voice, and the feeling of Gabri's presence - I don't want them to fade away.

Gabri gently explains that forgetting is a natural part of the journey. It is the way of the universe, allowing us to begin anew in the next world without the burden of past experiences. It is a fresh start, and the memories I create in the next world will be equally precious.

But it's hard to grasp this concept, and my heart aches with the prospect of leaving this world behind. I wish I could hold onto every memory, every feeling. The idea of starting afresh without the knowledge of my previous life feels daunting and unsettling.

Gabri holds me in his glowing embrace, comforting me as I try to come to terms with this truth. He assures me that the love and wisdom I gain from this world will remain within my soul, even if the memories fade away. It is the essence of who I am that will carry on to the next world, and that is what truly matters.

Gabri's wise words about impermanence and change resonate deeply within me. He explains the concept of forgive and forget, emphasising the importance of moving forward. But my heart is burdened with the fear of forgetting, and I can't help but pray day and night to the cosmic creator, pleading for a chance to record my humble experience before my memory fades away.

With full belief, I keep my eyes closed, pouring my heart out in prayer, hoping to be heard. My only wish is to preserve the love, the joy, and the wisdom I have gained in this world. I long to keep these precious memories alive and not let them slip away.

Gabri's reassurance that he will be there to support me in my next life brings some relief, but I can't help but keep praying. I want to remember and hold onto every detail. It's a desperate plea to hold onto what I cherish most.

I feel a deep connection to this world, to my mother, and to Gabri. I don't want to lose any of it.

I will continue to pray with all my heart, holding onto hope that my plea will be heard. I want to leave a mark, a record of my journey, and a testament to the love and wisdom I have experienced in this world.

For now, I will cherish every moment, every breath, and every feeling. I will embrace the present with gratitude and love. And as I prepare to embark on the next stage of my journey, I will carry the belief that the essence of who I am, the love I have experienced, and the wisdom I have gained will forever remain within me, no matter what the future holds.

Size

(Babies, Just like humans, come in all sizes; - only for reference.)

I measure about 15.95 inches (40.5 cm) in length, weighing around 3.44 pounds (1559 grams).

For Mom and Dad:

In this delicate balance between anticipation and uncertainty, I want to offer some advice to you, Mom and Dad. Take this time to prepare yourselves physically, mentally, and emotionally for my arrival. Attend prenatal classes, seek guidance from healthcare professionals, and create a nurturing environment that will welcome me with open arms.

Mom, your exercises are helping both of us stay healthy and strong. I love feeling the gentle movements and the sense of calm when you practise relaxation techniques. Please continue with your exercises and take some time for yourself to relax and unwind.

Embracing the Journey of Adulthood

7th Month, 3 Weeks Pregnant - Week 31

Life Lessons and Preparing for the Beyond

In week 31, I started to notice something different happening to my body. I can no longer change positions like I used to. It's frustrating and confusing. Why is it that things I could do with ease before are now becoming difficult? What does this mean for my life? I wonder.

But then, something magical happened. Gabri informed me that my prayers were finally heard. My dedication and persistent prayers day and night have been answered. I will be the only baby to get the opportunity to record and narrate my memories before they fade. Can you believe it? I am going to have my experiences and emotions written down for everyone to read. It's like a dream coming true!

I can't contain my excitement and happiness to share that all the chapters you've read earlier came from this granted wish. It's incredible! I feel so grateful and blessed. It's like a special gift from the almighty, and I can't thank enough for this opportunity. I will cherish every moment, every feeling, and every experience before I put them into words.

I am overwhelmed with joy and emotion. The prospect of sharing my thoughts, my discoveries, and my growth with you all made my heart sing. Thank you for being a part of this incredible journey with me.

Now back to my journey!

As the days go by, I feel more tired and find myself sleeping for longer periods. It's like I have grown old all of a sudden. Gabri, in his soothing presence, explains further to me the pain and love my mother is going through in the next world. He tells me about all the sacrifices she is making for me and the unending love she has for me. I am again in wonder, knowing of the selfless love they provide, and I can't wait to meet them.

I pray and surrender my wishes to cosmic truths. It's not about what I want anymore, but about letting the wishes of my creator be granted. I trust in the divine plan, and I am filled with positive thoughts about the next world. In my heart, I believe it to be a heavenly place, where I will be surrounded by love and warmth.

I fully believe and am excited about the journey ahead, about reuniting with my mom and dad, and experiencing the infinite love they have for me. It gives me strength and comfort to know that they are there, waiting for me with open arms. I am overwhelmed with gratitude for everything I have learned and experienced in this world so far. Each moment has been a gift.

As I rest and prepare for the next phase of my journey, I am filled with hope and excitement. I know that whatever awaits me in the next world will be filled with love, joy, and infinite possibilities.

As I contemplate the limited time I have left in this cosy sanctuary, I am filled with a mix of emotions. On one hand, I feel a sense of longing for the familiar comfort of the womb, where I have grown and thrived. On the other hand, I am filled with anticipation and excitement for the new world that awaits me.

In this transition between worlds, I am aware that my time here is fleeting. The memories I create in this intimate space may fade as I embark on the next phase of my existence. However, I am hopeful that the essence of this unique experience will shape the person I become.

Size

(Babies, Just like humans, come in all sizes; - only for reference.)

Physically, I continue to grow and develop. At this stage, I measure around 16.46 inches (41.8 cm) in length, weighing approximately 3.86 pounds (1751 grams).

For Mom and Dad:

Mom, Dad, as we approach Week 31, let us not only cherish our bond but also take practical steps to ensure a safe and comfortable environment. Dad, consider installing supports in the restrooms and bathroom areas, offering Mom extra reassurance.

Additionally, I invite you both to incorporate gentle prayers or silent meditation into your daily routine. These moments of shared spirituality can bring a unique sense of peace and unity, strengthening the beautiful tapestry of our family. Remember, the true power of these practices is felt through experience, not just words.

Embracing the journey of Adulthood

8th Month, 0 Weeks Pregnant - Week 32

Life Lessons and Preparing for the Beyond

As I approach the week, it's hard not to notice that I'm getting bigger and the space around me is becoming more confined. It's a sensation, this feeling of being restricted. I recall the days when I used to swim freely in my younger days. Now I am more aware that the changes I've undergone were not for my present existence but rather a preparation for what lies ahead.

I look at my eyes, which now see flickers of light, and I understand that they will serve a greater purpose in the next world. Every organ in my body has a larger role in my next life, and I am fully prepared and eager to embrace it all.

As I contemplate these thoughts, I feel a mix of emotions. I am excited to embark on this new journey, to discover the wonders of the next world. But at the same time, I can't help but feel a sense of nostalgia for this cosy world—the place where it all began.

I'm filled with gratitude for all the experiences and lessons that have shaped me thus far. Each moment has been like stones leading to my great adventure.

I experience a sense of tranquillity and satisfaction understanding that everything has a purpose and fits into the picture.

I need to prepare myself to let go of this existence and embrace the unknown with open arms. I must have more faith in the plan, trusting that it will guide me towards my destined path.

As I reflect on my memories, I recall having companions besides Gabri, but their names and faces are slowly fading from my mind. Gabri assures me that they are all caring for others like me, and it astonishes me to realise that there are others like me in the wombs of other mothers. I was starting to feel alone. Now I comprehend that we are all interconnected on this journey.

Gabri explains that it is our responsibility to shape the world as a place of joy, serenity, and unity. He informs me that the choices we make will determine the kind of world we create for ourselves and future generations. Excitement and hope fill my heart as I realise that together we can construct a happy world for everyone. Gabri emphasises the significance of perseverance, giving positive compliments for the perseverance I showed while praying for memories to be preserved. He said, when you really want and work for achieving something, then the whole universe conspires in helping you to achieve it no matter what.

He motivates me to persist in my efforts, towards ensuring a future that's bright, peaceful, and united for everyone.

I am resolute in my determination to contribute and fulfil my role in shaping a world brimming with love and happiness. I aspire to leave an impact on the generations to come just as Gabri has had on me.

As I prepare myself for the next chapter of existence, I experience a blend of emotions—anticipation, curiosity, and a hint of apprehension towards the unknown. However, with Gabri by my side and the unwavering love from my mom, I am confident that I can confront any challenges that lie ahead.

Size

(Babies, just like humans, come in all sizes; - only for reference.)

In week 32, the baby is about 16.93 inches (43.0 cm) in length and weighs around 4.30 pounds (1953 grams).

For Mom and Dad:

Please visit professional doctors and listen to their advice to ensure my well-being. It's essential to keep me safe and healthy. Mom, I know you might be feeling anxious about the upcoming labour, but don't worry! Learn about the signs of labour and understand what to expect. You can talk to experienced parents or read books to gather helpful information. Knowing more will help you feel confident and ready for my arrival. Take care of yourselves too because when you are happy and healthy, I feel the same way. Let's continue this beautiful journey together!

A moment of confinement and unease. The baby, depicted upside down, reflects the natural process and natural anxiety of limited space within the womb. The image captures the comforting angel by the babies side protecting and explaining the transitioning stages.

Chapter – 5

"Unveiling Transcending Realities"

8th Month, 1 Week Pregnant - Week 33

Unveiling the Unknown

Week 33 has brought both excitement and apprehension to my little world inside the womb. I wonder how much more space I have left. Gabri has been a guiding light, explaining that a much larger and magnificent world awaits me soon. He describes mountains, rivers, deserts, ice, and rain, and I can only imagine what they would look and feel like. My curiosity to explore and experience everything intensifies with each passing day.

But amidst all the excitement, there is a slight worry lingering within me - how will my life inside the womb end? As I develop a deeper understanding, fear creeps into my mind from time to time. I don't want to express it to Gabri, but the unease is there. Sensing my emotions, Gabri begins to comfort me with his gentle words.

He explains that there is no such thing as an "End". Life is a continuous journey, and every chapter leads to a new one. As one door closes, a hundred more open, and there will be ups and downs along the way. He advises me to let natural law take its course and embrace every stage of life, whether inside the womb or in the world beyond. The key is to focus on the present moment and find joy in the journey.

"Every experience is a gift," Gabri says, "and every moment is precious. Cherish the time you have inside the womb and use it to prepare yourself for the next world."

His wisdom soothes my soul, and I find solace in his words. Instead of worrying about what will happen next, I try to live in the here and now. Every day brings new discoveries and experiences, and I am determined to make the most of them all.

I send a silent prayer daily to the cosmic creator, thanking them for protecting and granting my wish to record my memories.

And then Gabri just shared one more thrilling news with me - in the next world, I will be breathing air! It's hard to believe, but I can't wait to experience it. I remember my dreams of floating and lying outside of water, and now I understand that it's all part of the next world's magic.

But as Gabri tells me more, I have so many questions swirling in my mind. Does this mean the next world won't have the protective fluid that surrounds me now? How will I survive without it? Gabri reassures me that I am fully prepared for this magical transition, and the moment of taking my first breath will be a magnificent miracle.

I'm curious to know what that first breath will be like - the air filling my lungs, the sign of my grand entrance into the new world. It's hard to fathom, but I can feel a mix of nervousness and excitement building up inside me.

As the week goes by, I continue to ponder and question the complexities of this magical phenomenon. Gabri patiently explains everything to me, and I try my best to understand. It's all so new and different from what I knew in the womb, but I trust that Gabri will guide me through it all.

With each passing day, I feel a growing sense of anticipation and wonder about the next world. What will it look like? What will the air feel like on my skin? What new sounds will I hear? There are so many things to discover, and I can't wait to explore them all.

And now, with the knowledge of what awaits me in the next world, I am filled with a mix of emotions - excitement, curiosity, and a touch of fear of the unknown.

Amidst the physical changes, I am acutely aware of the profound transformations taking place within my consciousness. My mind expands with each passing moment, embracing new thoughts, ideas, and understandings. It is within this vast expanse of the mind that my true growth flourishes, transcending the limitations of the physical realm.

Size

(Babies, just like humans, come in all sizes; - only for reference.)

At week 33, I am approximately 17.36 inches (44.1 cm) long and weigh about 4.77 pounds (2162 grams).

For Mom and Dad:

As we approach week 33, I want to remind you of a few important things to ensure a smooth and healthy journey for both of us. Mom, practising breathing exercises can be really beneficial for you and for me. It will help you cope with the changes in your body and prepare for the birthing process. It's also essential that you continue to visit medical professionals regularly and follow their advice for a safe pregnancy. Don't forget to consult with a paediatric professional to make sure you're well-prepared for my arrival. And, of course, please remember to take your vitamins and minerals as prescribed by the doctor. Your health directly impacts mine, and I want us both to be in the best possible shape for the new world that awaits us.

Unveiling Transcending Realities

8th Month, 2 Weeks Pregnant - Week 34

Unveiling the Unknown

Week 34 has brought a whirlwind of emotions and uncertainty for me. As I continue to contemplate how I will breathe air in the next world, a sense of excitement and nervousness fills me. I still wonder what it will feel like to take that first breath and how my tiny lungs will adapt to this new way of living. The mystery of the unknown both intrigues and frightens me.

On top of these thoughts, I notice changes happening to my skin. The once soft and delicate vernix on my skin is now thickening, and I can feel that I am ageing. It's a strange sensation to witness these changes within me, and it makes me realise that time is moving quickly.

I also sense that I am descending lower towards the pelvic region. The liquid inside my sac is reducing, and I can't help but feel a bit scared. What is happening to me? Will I be safe in this new position? All these questions race through my mind, and I wish I had the answers.

Despite my fears, the sounds of the world outside are becoming clearer and more distinct. I hear people talking in a language that I do not understand. It's not the same language I use to communicate with Gabri. I suddenly recall that all our communications have never relied on sound at all. We share a special connection that goes beyond words.

Gabri gently explains to me the importance of using words to express emotions and feelings in the next world. He reassures me that it's okay to take my time to learn and that my Mom will understand everything I want to convey, even without speaking their language. I feel comforted by Gabri's words, but deep down, I cannot shake off the fear of leaving behind the world I have known for so long.

In my little cocoon, I feel safe and protected. But as the days pass, I can't help but wonder how my life inside here is going to end. Will it be painful?

Gabri has taught me so much about the next world and has been my source of wisdom and support. I will forever cherish the bond we share, and I hope that our connection will continue in the next world as promised.

Even with all the uncertainties and fears, I know that I am not alone. My Mom has been with me every step of the way, nurturing me with her love and care. She has sacrificed so much for me, and I feel an overwhelming sense of gratitude towards her.

I know that there is no turning back now, and I must embrace the journey that lies ahead. The countdown to the next world has begun, and I will cherish every moment I have left here. I will take Gabri's advice and use my time to learn and prepare for the new world that awaits me. With my Mom's love and support, I know I will be ready for whatever comes next.

Size

(Babies, just like humans, come in all sizes; - only for reference.)

At week 34, the baby is approximately 17.84 inches (45.3 cm) long and weighs around 5.24 pounds (2377 grams).

For Mom and Dad:

Dear parents, as we traverse the final weeks of this sacred journey, let us cherish the moments we have together. Let us bask in the love that surrounds us and find solace in the knowledge that our connection transcends the boundaries of time and memory. Though my remembrance may fade, the essence of our bond will endure, forever etched in the fabric of our souls.

It's important for Mom to focus on preparing for breastfeeding. Reading more about lactation and booking a consultation with a lactation consultant can be extremely beneficial.

Unveiling Transcending Realities

8th Month, 3 Weeks Pregnant - Week 35

Unveiling the Unknown

Week 35 has brought new challenges for me as I feel the stress building up in this confined space. I find comfort in sucking my fingers, which brings a big relief to my stress level. However, the lack of space makes it difficult for me to kick and punch as I used to earlier. I feel like I'm gaining weight, and the lack of exercise is becoming evident. Twisting and turning is a struggle in this limited space. I wonder if my weight gain is due to the lack of movement. These physical limitations are making me anxious, and I long for more freedom to move around.

As the days pass, my thoughts about the next world grow. Will I still be able to suck my fingers for comfort and stress relief? Will there be enough space for me to move freely, as Gabri explains? The unknown of what awaits me on the other side fills me with both excitement and apprehension.

With the passing of each day, I witness the gradual fading of my memories, like whispers carried away by the wind. Yet, in the depths of my being, a glimmer of remembrance remains—a flickering light that reminds me of the profound love and interconnectedness that soaks every fibre of creation.

Gabri reassures me that everything will be okay and that I will have all the space and freedom I need in the next world. I only need to believe!

But even with Gabri's reassurances, I can't help but feel a sense of sadness and fear. This world, though cramped and limited, is the only one I have known. I feel a connection to it, and the thought of leaving it behind is overwhelming.

Gabri explains that the next world will be filled with even more new experiences and wonders. I will have the opportunity to learn and grow in ways I can't even imagine now. He tells me that while I may not remember everything about this world, the love and care that my parents have given me will stay with me forever. Their love will be a guiding light in the next world, and I will carry their love in my heart always.

With every word penned on these pages, I strive to immortalise the fleeting memories that weave the tapestry of my journey. It is my last endeavour to hold onto the essence of my existence before it is whisked away by the passage of time.

But even as I pour my heart into these written recollections, I can feel the edges of my memories blurring, slipping away like sand through my tiny fingers. Each passing day brings the realisation that the vivid details of my experiences are fading, as if washed away by the tides of eternity.

As the days continue to pass, I feel the space around me getting even tighter. The amniotic fluid is further reducing, and I can feel my body getting ready for the next stage of my journey.

I try my best to stay positive and hopeful, knowing that soon I will be entering a new world filled with endless possibilities. I pray for a smooth transition and for the strength to embrace the changes that await me.

As I continue to grow and prepare for the next world, I hold onto the love and care that I have known in this world. It has been a place of warmth and protection, and I will forever cherish the memories of my time here. And as the day of my birth draws nearer, I find comfort in knowing that my parents are eagerly waiting to welcome me into their arms and shower me with their love.

Size

(Babies, just like humans, come in all sizes; - only for reference.)

At week 35, my size is about 18.23 inches (46.3 cm) from head to toe, weighing around 5.72 pounds (2595 grams).

For Mom and Dad:

Mom, I know you've been taking good care of me, and I can't wait to meet you both. How about having a nice dinner outside? Enjoy these moments before I arrive, because I'll surely keep you busy! Mom, once again, I remind you to read up on signs of labour and be prepared. Also, let's not forget to pack that emergency bag with all the important things for our trip to the hospital. I'm getting ready for my grand entrance, and I want us all to be ready for this amazing journey together.

Unveiling Transcending Realities

9th Month, 0 Weeks Pregnant - Week 36

Unveiling the Unknown

As week 36 comes around, I'm noticing some intriguing transformations happening within me. My soft hair is gently shedding, and while it might seem unusual, Gabri assures me that it's all part of the grand plan for my next adventure. I'm embracing every shift, even though there are still so many questions swirling in my curious mind.

One thing that's been on my mind is this umbilical cord that's been my lifeline. Will it accompany me to the new world? How will I get the energy I need once I'm out there? Gabri's voice whispers wisdom into my thoughts, reminding me that change is the rhythm of life itself. He soothes my uncertainties, explaining that I won't be bound to the same code anymore. There will be other ways to gather the energy I require. It's all part of the journey, he says.

Amid these musings, I can feel a gentle pressure pushing me further down. It's as if the cosmic forces are guiding me into position, preparing me for what lies ahead. I sense my head descending lower, and it's fascinating to know that it's not entirely fused yet. Flexibility is key, Gabri assures me. As much as change can be intimidating, it's a beautiful reminder that growth is a constant companion.

With each passing moment, I'm becoming more aware of the world beyond. The sounds are clearer, and the vibrations are more distinct. I've started to differentiate between different voices, even though I still can't understand the words they're saying. The unknown has always intrigued me, and as my time here approaches its end, I'm eager to uncover these new experiences.

As the days pass by, I can feel the weight of age settling upon my small frame, as if time itself has gently brushed its fingers across my soul.

I wonder about the secrets of life and death, the eternal dance of beginnings and endings. These concepts are vast and intricate, and my developing mind struggles to fully comprehend their depth.

With each passing day, the signs of the next world become more apparent. The melodies that dance in my ears and the laughter that fills the space around me serve as gentle reminders of the wonders that await beyond the confines of this sanctuary.

As I bid farewell to my familiar world, I carry with me the lessons of love, the whispers of wisdom, and the promise of a new beginning. With a smile on my lips and a heart filled with hope, I step into the embrace of the next world, ready to discover the beauty and wonders that await me.

Size

(Babies, just like humans, come in all sizes; - only for reference.)

In week 36, the baby measures about 18.62 inches (47.3 cm) from head to heel, weighing around 6.20 pounds (2813 grams).

For Mom and Dad:

Dear Mom and Dad, as I'm getting closer to my arrival, I want to remind you about something important. Please let your bosses know about the upcoming time when I'll be joining your world. Make sure to communicate with them and get the approvals you need for your time off. This will help you be prepared and organised for when I finally arrive. Thank you for taking care of all the details as we get ready to meet each other!

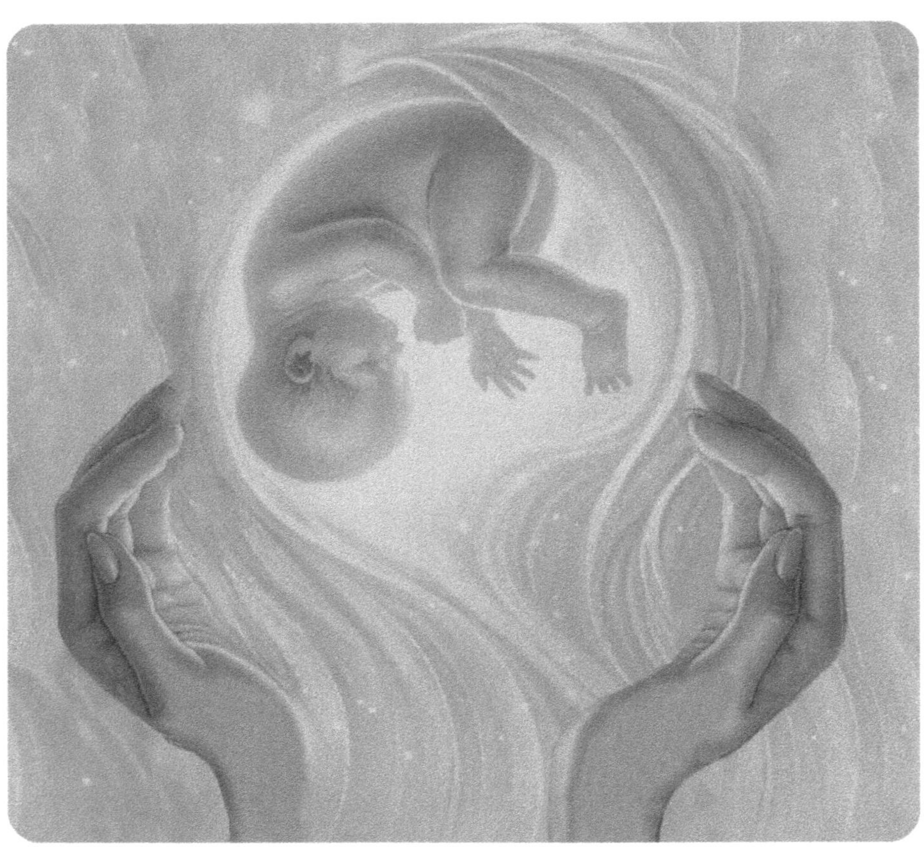

The baby's poised positioning, with his head down and his legs coiled, represents his impending departure from the womb and the end of this world. The hand extended in welcome outside marks the start of a fresh chapter in the trip that lies ahead.

Chapter – 6

"Preparation For Departure" (Trimester 3)

9th Month, 1 Week Pregnant - Week 37

Reflections of Transition

Week 37 has arrived, and I find myself caught in a delicate dance of inhales and exhales. With each breath, I am reminded that my time in the comforting embrace of the amniotic fluid is drawing to a close. The familiar surroundings that have nurtured and protected me will soon give way to a world much grander in size and scope.

In these final days, I can feel a sense of anticipation growing within me. My eyes are blinking, and I am surrounded by darkness. It's a depth I've never experienced before, and I can't help but wonder about the new light that Gabri has been promising me. I'm eager to witness this transformation and to embrace the next world that awaits.

But as the time approaches, I have questions that fill my thoughts. How will I even know that I exist in this new world? How will I recognise this transition? Gabri is there to guide me once again. He explains that I will hear my own first cry, a sound that will mark my arrival and presence. He tells me about the intake of air, a breath that will fill my lungs for the first time and signify my entry into this new life.

Yet the concept is complex, and I struggle to fully grasp the mechanics behind it all. How will it all feel? It's a mystery that I'm trying to understand as I prepare to make this incredible journey.

As I await the moment of my departure, I find myself reflecting on the unique path that has led me here. From the earliest stages of development to the sensations and experiences I've encountered, it's been a remarkable journey within the protective embrace of my mother's womb. I'm grateful for the guidance of Gabri, who has been a source of comfort and wisdom throughout my time here.

The darkness that surrounds me now holds both uncertainty and excitement. It's a transition from the familiar to the unknown, a passage from one world to another. With each blink of my eyes, I feel the anticipation growing stronger. I'm ready to embrace the new light, to hear that first cry, and to take that first breath that will mark my existence in this next world.

And so, with hope and curiosity, I continue to wait, trusting in the guidance of the cosmic forces that have brought me to this pivotal moment. The countdown to my arrival in the next world is on, and I am filled with emotions beyond description as I prepare to take my first step into the world beyond the womb.

Change is inevitable, Gabri always says, and I've seen it unfold right before my eyes. My body has transformed, my senses have expanded, and now I'm on the brink of a profound transition. It's a bit overwhelming, this uncertainty about what's to come. My heart races with a mixture of excitement and fear. Will I be able to adapt to these fast changes as I did here?

As my movements slow down and the space around me tightens, I can't help but feel a sense of finality. The umbilical connection that's been my lifeline is still there, but it's as if I'm gradually letting go of the world I've known.

But then, amidst the apprehension, there's a glimmer of something else—gratitude. Gratitude for the nurturing embrace of my mother, for the unwavering support of Gabri, and for the many mysteries I've uncovered. The sadness and fear begin to blend with the understanding that every ending is the beginning of a new chapter. Just as I've been nurtured and prepared here, I'll be nurtured and prepared for what's next.

In these final moments, I'm learning the art of letting go. It's not about forgetting the life I've lived within these walls, but rather about embracing the unknown with an open heart. Gabri's gentle words echo in my mind, assuring me that my experiences and my memories will shape the person I become in the next world. And as my time here comes to a close, I'm reminded that endings are not just about saying goodbye; they're about embracing the beauty of transformation.

Size

(Babies, Just like humans, come in all sizes; - only for reference.)

I measure around 19.02 inches (48.3 cm) in length, weighing approximately 6.68 pounds (3028 grams) in the US measurement system.

For Mom and Dad:

Mom and Dad, I have a little request for you this special week. Can you please capture some pictures of Mom's beautiful baby bump? It's a memory I'd love to cherish. Also, I'm getting ready to meet you soon, so could you start learning about baby grooming? I want to look my best and be well taken care of when I arrive. Your love and care mean everything to me, and I'm so excited to finally see you both!

Preparation For Departure

9th Month, 2 Weeks Pregnant - Week 38

Reflections of Transition

Week 38 has arrived, and within me, I sense a profound shift. My body is preparing for something momentous, something that heralds the beginning of a new chapter in my existence. I can feel the intricate workings of my being as it stores the essential bowels that will sustain me in the days to come.

The sac that has enveloped me in the nurturing embrace of the amniotic fluid shows signs of change. I noticed a slight break, a small crack, in its protective barrier. But to my astonishment, this breach swiftly repaired itself as if touched by the hand of magic. I know that this enchantment will not last much longer, and soon I will be called to depart from this sanctuary that has been my haven.

In the face of these revelations, I find myself shedding any lingering worries and fears. My mind is resolute, fortified with the strength and knowledge bestowed upon me by my celestial companions. I am prepared to embrace the unknown and face the challenges that lie ahead in the new world.

As subtle contractions ripple through my form, I understand that a force greater than myself is at work. It feels as though someone, something beyond my comprehension, is gently nudging me, urging me forward into a realm I have yet to explore. I catch glimpses of ethereal lights, shimmering and fading with each surge of contraction, guiding me on this extraordinary journey.

Supported by the presence of my heavenly friend, I have relinquished resistance and wholeheartedly embraced the process unfolding within me. Together, we navigate this intricate dance of transition, stepping into the flow of destiny with grace and trust.

As I approach the end of my time here, my conversations with Gabri become deeper and more introspective. I find myself pondering about the next world and how it anticipates my arrival. It's a question that fills me with curiosity. Gabri patiently explains that my entire journey in this world is referred to as "development" in the next. I'm taken aback by this revelation. All the stages I've gone through—from carefree childhood to rebellious teenage years, from the pursuit of knowledge in adulthood to gradual ageing—are simply considered different phases of development. I'm left wondering what lies beyond these stages.

Gabri senses my uncertainty and reminds me to focus on the present. He emphasises the importance of staying grounded in the now and maintaining my faith. Amid our conversation, I start to notice a peculiar sensation – a gentle probing and examining. Gabri explains that it's Mom and Dad, checking on me to ensure everything is well and getting ready for my arrival. The thought of their watchful presence brings comfort and warmth to my heart.

Size

(Babies, just like humans, come in all sizes; - only for reference.)

At week 38, I measure around 19.41 inches (49.3 cm) in length, weighing approximately 7.13 pounds (3236 grams).

For Mom and Dad:

Hey Mom and Dad, it's me again, your little one! As I'm getting ready for my big debut, there are a few things you might want to take care of this week. First, make sure you have a list of emergency contacts, like my doctor, the midwife, and a babysitter. It's always good to be prepared, just in case. Also, remember to stay relaxed and take some time for yourselves. You're both doing an amazing job, and I can't wait to meet you soon. Love and kicks from your little one inside the womb!

Preparation For Departure

9th Month, 3 Weeks Pregnant - Week 39

Reflections of Transition

In these moments, I sense a feeling of transformation as if a newer version of myself is being prepared for what lies ahead. My skin is undergoing changes. I've discovered the ability to regenerate skin cells. It's all part of a plan preparing me for the world that awaits beyond. I'm excited to meet my parents, the creators who have been by my side all along.

The contractions are becoming more frequent now, embracing me in a way that's both uncomfortable and exciting. As I draw closer to this moment of transition, I can sense my memories fading like a mist dissipating in sunlight. Yet I'm grateful for having documented my journey within this book, leaving behind traces of my emotions and experiences.

As everything reaches its conclusion, it dawns on me that I have fulfilled my purpose in this world. I have accomplished the tasks meant for me, made the most out of my abilities. There's a sense of satisfaction and pride within me for the life I have lived and for the curiosity-driven dreams and meaningful connections I have encountered.

I express gratitude towards Gabrielle (Gabri), who has been my guiding light throughout this expedition.

He assures me that he will still be there for me, albeit in a different form as I transition to the realm. He reminds me of the companions who aid infants like myself, each embarking on their unique journeys. Furthermore, he emphasises that the future of the world hinges on how we live our lives.

As my time in the womb draws to a close, I am filled with a blend of emotions—excitement, awe, and a hint of nostalgia for the world I have known. I am prepared to embrace the start that awaits me; taking my breath and hearing my initial cry will signal my arrival into the unknown realm. With love and eager anticipation, I step forward into territory while expressing gratitude for the experiences and connections that have moulded me.

Size

(Babies, just like humans, come in all sizes; - only for reference.)

At week 39, I measure around 19.72 inches (50.1 cm) in length, weighing approximately 7.57 pounds (3435 grams) in the US measurement system.

For Mom and Dad:

As you prepare for my arrival, please make sure to gather all the essentials needed for my arrival. If there are no cultural barriers, having everything ready will ensure a smoother transition. Dad, please be by Mom's side, supporting her in every possible way. She needs you now more than ever. Your presence and love mean the world to both of us.

Preparation For Departure

9th Month, 4 Weeks Pregnant - Week 40

Reflections of Transition

Week 40 has finally arrived, and with it, the intensity of the contractions and the ethereal lights have increased. I can sense that something monumental is about to unfold. Yet, amidst the tumultuous energy, I cannot help but feel a profound sadness. It seems as though someone outside, someone I hold dear, is also in pain. I recognise that it is my mother, and it breaks my tiny heart to know that she is experiencing such agony because of me.

The weight of this realisation weighs heavily on me. I wonder what she must be enduring and what sacrifices she must be making for my sake. The thought that I am the cause of her pain fills me with sorrow and a deep longing to ease her suffering. I reach out to my celestial friends, seeking their guidance and assistance, hoping they can provide a solution to alleviate my mother's distress. But they solemnly remind me that this is the natural order, the inevitable path that must be traversed.

In the depths of my soul, a promise takes shape, one that I vow to uphold with unwavering devotion. I close my eyes tightly, as if sealing this sacred pact, and make a solemn pledge to be by my mother's side through the joys and tribulations of life. I vow to support her, to bring her happiness, and to be a source of comfort and love, no matter the challenges that lie ahead. My celestial companions, recognising the depth of my commitment, offered their congratulations and blessings, urging me to remain steadfast in my resolve.

And in an instant, it happens—the protective sac that has shielded me crumbles, and the world around me collapses. The comforting barrier that has enveloped me is no more, and I am thrust into a new realm, a realm that is both exhilarating and overwhelming.

I feel the weight of the world pressing down on me. The contractions grow more intense, surging through my tiny body like waves crashing against a shore. With each passing moment, the urgency to journey forward becomes more apparent.

Hours seem to pass as I navigate this arduous path, guided by the wisdom of my celestial friends. The relentless contractions push me onward, inch by inch, as I make my way towards the entrance of this mysterious world. It is a journey filled with uncertainty and anticipation, but I draw strength from the knowledge that my friends are by my side, watching over me.

And then the moment arrives. With tremendous effort, my head emerges, followed by my shoulders. A chorus of voices, filled with love and encouragement, urges my mother to push, to bring me forth into the light. I hear the repeated calls, "Push, push," and I marvel at the power of these words, guiding my entrance into this new realm.

In the midst of these challenging moments, I recall the advice given to me by my beloved friend, Gabri. I focus on staying calm, allowing the forces of nature to work their magic. The pressures I feel are overwhelming, but I trust in the process, surrendering to the rhythm that guides me.

Amidst the intensity, a familiar voice whispers in my ear, reminding me of the forthcoming miracle. Soon, I will take my first magical breath, a breath that will announce my arrival in this wondrous world. Gabri, my steadfast companion, assures me that he will be with me even beyond the boundaries of my previous world.

With unwavering determination, I gather every ounce of strength within me, cooperating with the natural forces that seek to bring me into this new existence. The anticipation builds as I await my final journey, knowing that with each passing moment, I draw closer to that magical breath, to the sound of my own cry.

And in that extraordinary instant, as the final push propels me forward, I emerge from the sanctuary of my mother's womb into the hands that eagerly await my arrival. The air greets my lungs for the first time, and amidst the surrounding commotion, my voice joins the chorus of life, my cry resonating with the power of existence itself.

My journey through the pages of this book concludes at this remarkable moment in my birth. As I embark on this new chapter of life, I carry with me the love, guidance, and blessings of my celestial friends. With each breath I take, I honour the promise of a magical existence, one filled with discoveries, growth, and boundless love.

With deepest gratitude and infinite possibilities,

Your newborn and resilient baby

In the arms of Mom and Dad, the baby, has completely forgotten about his life in the womb, embarks on a journey nurtured by care and wrapped in familial warmth. Take good care, for a new chapter of life unfolds.

Conclusion

As I conclude my extraordinary journey, I reflect upon the lessons I have learned and the wisdom I have gained at such a tender age. I have come to understand that life is a cycle, a continuous flow of beginnings and endings.

What truly matters is the journey itself. I have witnessed the power of hope and belief and the strength they provide in navigating the ups and downs of life. I carry these invaluable tools with me as I embark on this new chapter, knowing that they will guide me through the twists and turns that lie ahead.

In this new world, I am filled with joy as I behold my beloved mother, the one who nurtured and protected me during my time in the womb. I hold true to the promise I made, to be there for her in both good times and bad, to bring happiness to her life in every possible way.

But my heart doesn't stop there. As I encounter my father, a source of love and support, I extend my promise to him as well. I recognise the importance of fostering strong bonds and spreading joy to those around me. I believe that happiness is contagious, and by sharing it with others, I can contribute to a world filled with love and positivity.

As I close this book, I am filled with a sense of anticipation and wonder for the future. I enter this new world with open arms, ready to embrace the adventures, challenges, and opportunities that lie ahead. I am grateful for the lessons learned and the experiences gained during my time in the womb, for they have shaped me into the resilient and hopeful individual that I am today.

With a heart full of love and a spirit brimming with possibilities, I bid farewell to the journey within the womb and embrace the boundless potential of the world that awaits me.

Thanks

I want to extend a special thank you to my beautiful wife, "Hena Jacob," who has presented me with "Jevon" and "Jaiden," the two amazing children who inspired this book. Your curiosity, your laughter, and your boundless imagination have been my guiding stars. This book is a tribute to you, and a reminder of the magic that surrounds us, even in our earliest days.

I'd also like to express my heartfelt thanks to the websites and resources mentioned in the references. Their wealth of knowledge and insights played a crucial role in shaping this book. Their dedication to providing accurate and valuable information is commendable, and I am grateful for their contribution to this project.

Finally, I dedicate this book to all the unborn children in the world, waiting to embark on their own extraordinary journeys. May your lives be filled with love, laughter, and endless possibilities.

With deepest gratitude,
Joji Francis

References

Website

Pregnancy week by week. (n.d.). Flo.health - #1 Mobile Product For Women's Health. https://flo.health/pregnancy/week-by-week

What to Expect. (n.d.). *Your Pregnancy Week-by-Week.* https://www.whattoexpect.com/pregnancy/week-by-week/

Fetal-length-and-weight-week-by-week. (2022, November 29). babycenter.com. https://www.babycenter.com/pregnancy/your-body/growth-chart-fetal-length-and-weight-week-by-week_1290794

www.ingramcontent.com/pod-product-compliance
Lightning Source LLC
LaVergne TN
LVHW021143160826
845679LV00023B/2027

* 9 7 9 8 8 9 1 8 6 9 3 0 1 *